Mel Massey

Decker

A Companion Novel to the Earth's Magick Series

DECKER

A COMPANION NOVEL TO THE EARTH'S MAGICK SERIES

Cover Art:
Dustin Compton

www.IllustratedNightmares.com.

Publisher's Note:

This is a work of fiction. All names, characters, places, and
events are the work of the author's imagination.

Any resemblance to real persons, places, or events is
coincidental.

Solstice Publishing - www.solsticepublishing.com

Copyright 2014

Mel Massey

Dedication

Many thanks and much love to the members of the Elementai Secret Society, without you this wouldn't be as much fun. I love and appreciate all of you.

Thank you to The Monster I Married for tolerating me when I spend so much time in my imaginary world.

And lastly, for Decker…now you're real.

The Earth's Magick Series:

Earth's Magick, Book 1 ~Earth~

Decker – A Companion Novel to the Earth's Magick Series

Earth's Magick, Book 2 ~Water~ - Coming soon

Chapter One

The light from the fire made the back of Mela's house dance with shadows. Decker sat on the back porch smoking a cigarette while he stared off into the night. He took a drag and tilted his head back to exhale the smoke. His ever-present black bowler hat sat on one knee, the other leg stretched out before him.

He righted his head, tilting it slightly to the side as Wyatt approached. His yellow catlike eyes never moved as they searched the darkness. He could hear Wyatt's steps but it was his smell that shouted his presence in the darkness. Decker knew everyone's smells the way others knew the sound of a voice.

"Oy, what you doing out here?" Decker quietly asked. Everyone had gone to sleep, or so he thought.

"Hey there, Decker. I was wondering," Wyatt grabbed a patio chair and noisily moved it until it sat right next to Decker's. "I was wondering if we could talk."

"Talk? What for? About what?" Confused, he faced Wyatt and frowned. "What'd I do?"

"Nothing," Wyatt laughed. "I had an idea and I wanted to run it past you. You know, see what you think." Decker's eyes narrowed and he nodded his head for Wyatt to continue. "I think this is a fantastic idea. I want you and the others to tell me your stories. You know, like dictate your memoirs to me. I take good notes, and I also want to record it, to make sure I get it right. What do you think?"

"Why?" Decker growled.

"Because, you brute, you're fascinating! The history and the stories you could tell are like nothing we've ever heard before." Wyatt's charming smile never withered under Decker's glare.

"Why don't you ask Vasha? He likes to talk about things like feelings and he's better at remembering stuff. Why you asking me?"

"Well, you're the most important one, aren't you? Shhh…don't tell anyone I said that, though." He brought his voice down to a whisper. Decker fidgeted in his chair for a moment and wrestled with the desire to tell Wyatt to go to hell. He didn't want to talk about the past. The past was better left alone to fade into nothingness. But there were things he knew that would not only be interesting but possibly helpful as well.

"What kind of questions?" he asked finally as he tossed his cigarette into the yard.

"Easy ones. I ask the questions and you just talk till you can't talk anymore."

Decker shrugged and waved his hand for Wyatt to go ahead. He eyed Wyatt as he lit another cigarette, silently watching him produce a small recorder from his back pocket, and a pad of paper.

"This is Wyatt recording the life and times of Dektrios, otherwise known as Decker to his friends." He cleared his throat a few times and flipped through his notebook until he found the page he was looking for. Decker's eyebrows raised but he said nothing. "Decker, how old are you? When and where were you born?"

"That's three questions in one, mate. I've got a general idea, but not exact. A long time ago, I was able to figure it pretty close. We didn't keep records the way your lot does now." He gestured toward the recorder in Wyatt's hand. "We told stories over and over until we remembered them and then passed them along to other people. That's how my people worked."

"What were you able to figure out?"

"I'm trying to tell you, if you give me a moment, thank you very much. I was able to do some simple arithmetic once and came up with my approximate age of two thousand three hundred years."

"Seriously? You were born before Jesus?" Wyatt's hazel eyes were wide with excitement.

"Bugger it all….yes. I was born before your Jesus. Now, back to me. My tribe, well, it wasn't really mine, was it? We never belonged to that bunch of ingrates. But, for the sake of this conversation, our people were from the Arabian tribal lands. Now, it's the country of Saudi Arabia. Fuck, things were different then. Really different." He took another drag from his cigarette and slowly blew the smoke into the air. "Basra. The nearest place that would show on a map was Basra. There was a market there where merchants brought their goods to trade."

"Did you ever go?"

"Yeah. Yeah, I went a few times with…with my sisters, Akasma and Aydan. We would go to the markets for things we needed. Material for clothes, food, incense too. There was a huge area in the market just for incense. The smell was lovely. Sometimes, Mela will light some of her incense sticks and I remember things…"

"Smells always make me remember things too. That's common for people, I think." Wyatt's voice trailed off and he gave Decker a small smile. "Sorry. Go on."

"Bah, it was such a long time ago. Why you want me to go back this far? I could tell you about my time as a soldier of Rome." Wyatt waved him off and shook his head.

"Nope. I want the whole story. No cheating, Decker. I ask and you answer, that's what we agreed on."

"Camels."

"What?" Wyatt asked, taken off guard.

"Camels. There were a lot of camels everywhere. People used them for traveling and for carrying their stuff. Smelly and noisy creatures, to be sure. When we went go to market, Akasma would borrow camels from a family in the village who were kind. Not many were, mind you. Even less then than now, I think." Decker sat back and stared off into the night again as he continued.

"We would walk through the market streets, the girls all wrapped up in their scarves. I did the same then but we men only wore one on our head to keep the sun off. I was there to protect them, see. My sisters were beautiful and I had to protect them…"

"Did anyone ever notice that you were…different?"

Decker sat for a moment, lost in his deep well of memories, when suddenly he let out a bark of laughter.

"Oh sure." He chuckled again. "Oh yeah. Once, when we were leaving the market, a group of men came up behind us. They said how lovely the sky was and how lovely the views were. Then, they said there were two lovely maidens there that made it all the better. My sisters didn't react, they simply kept going forward. But me, I listened well to them while they discussed my sisters with their filthy mouths and their stinking bodies that craved them. They smelled like stale wine and camel shit. It didn't take long for them to overstep their bounds neither. They rode up beside us and tried to grab the reigns of Akasma's camel. They paid me no mind because I was smaller then, but stronger than they were, even young as I was."

"Oh my God, did you kill them?" Wyatt couldn't help but ask. Decker seemed to enjoy the question and he smiled.

"The man pleaded with my sisters to stop and to sit with them on their camels. When they said no, the men surrounded us and stood in our way. What else could I do? It was my duty to watch over the girls. They brought me along to protect them, after all. The one that grabbed Akasma's reins lost an arm. With one slice from my sword, it plopped right to the ground." He laughed at the memory.

"Yuck. You and chopping off body parts."

Decker howled with laughter. "It was bloody glorious." He stood up and held his arm as if he were the wounded man and made a terrible grimace of pain. "My arm! My arm! You cut it off!" he mimicked. "It was beautiful. The other men drew short swords on me and thought they could rush me."

"They couldn't take you, could they?" Wyatt asked, enthralled by the tale.

"Hell no, they couldn't. But it didn't even come to that. My sisters sat like statues on their camels and I hopped off mine to the howling man with one arm. I picked up his bloody stump and hit him with it." Wyatt made a face of disgust and Decker laughed again. "It made a wet noise when it hit his face. I beat the man with his own arm. That's a beautiful, and rare thing, make no mistake. The others, seeing a crazy, wild boy wielding a severed arm as a weapon, decided to turn around and leave."

"Smart of them," Wyatt sat with his hand almost covering his mouth.

"Yeah. Real smart. I turned to the man on the ground and pointed his own hand at his face. I told him, 'Sir, you have no honor and for that, you have lost an arm. Follow us no more or you will lose the other one!'" He sat back down and searched for his pack of cigarettes. "The one-armed man sat on the ground and nodded his head, begging me to spare his life. I did. See, I can be very merciful."

"Full of mercy."

"Judge not, Wyatt. Those were the times we lived in then. Had I not been there, the girls would have been raped and their throats slit open. No one travelled alone in those days." Decker lit another cigarette and smiled.

"I'm not judging, Decker. It's just gross that you like to cut off body parts all the time."

Decker stretched his legs in front of him and took a drag from his cigarette. His yellow eyes focused again on the darkness beyond the firelight. Wyatt wanted him to talk more but the expression on his face forced him keep his silence. Decker wasn't seeing the trees or the fire, but people from very long ago. He was remembering their faces. He was remembering how they spoke. He was remembering they were all dead.

"The girls loved it," Decker's voice was almost a whisper. "They loved to go to the markets and see all of the people and the stacked pottery. I don't know why they bought that stuff. We lived in a cave that was full of dust and bugs. But they would spend all day cleaning up the dirt and moving rugs here to there..." His voice trailed off.

"It sounds like they were trying to make a home for you and your brothers." Wyatt said softly. Decker nodded, still lost in his memories. Wyatt cleared his throat to try and bring him back.

"What else you want know?" Wyatt smiled and checked his papers. He made a quick notation on the paper and looked back at Decker. "Well...I was wondering if you could tell me about....Him. The man that came to take you and your brothers away. Sammuele called him The Darkness in human form. Can you tell me a little about that time?"

Decker stared at him for a long moment and considered the question.

"We were older by that time. Azul was almost to his full size." He pointed his cigarette at Wyatt. "An impressive size, mind you. As tall as this house. I remember Azul spent many nights alone then. He was too big to be left in the cave all the time. Azul needed to fly."

"Wait. Azul...the scary one...he flies?" Fear made Wyatt's face pale. Lately he has seen many things but everyone spoke of Azul as something to fear with a level of seriousness that frightened him.

"Aye, he flies. He would hunt and come back before sunrise. I remember...he changed then. He stopped speaking to us and slept all day. When the sun fell below the horizon, he would get up and swoop right out the cave without a word. The girls, they would worry and try to make him happy when he returned. They would make him things, hang a new garland of flowers for him but he stopped caring." Decker tossed his cigarette into the yard and crossed his arms over his chest.

"That's when you knew something was going on?"

"No. Not me. I just figured he was tired of being cooped up. We all were. But it was when he asked Vasha, Theo and I to come with him that I knew something was different. He'd never done that before. The girls knew but pretended not to notice us leaving the cave together one night. I rode on Azul's back while Vasha and Theo, who got longer legs than me, kept pace with him. He took us to the little river that flowed next to our cave. I remember seeing the stars in the sky and the moon was waxing that night."

"Was He there?"

"Usually I can sense stuff, I can smell others around. But this one, he had no smell. He came from behind a tree and smiled at us."

"What did he look like?" Wyatt's curiosity got the better of him.

"He wore the same sort of robes those in the village wore. His hair was brown and he wore sandals on his feet. Nothing made him special except..."

"Except what?" Wyatt didn't have the patience to keep quiet any longer.

"His damned eyes. They were black and bigger than they should've been. You see my eyes, Wyatt?" Decker leaned into Wyatt's face and stared with his yellow catlike eyes. Wyatt nodded. "Mine are like an animal's eyes but his...his eyes weren't natural. You get my meaning?" Wyatt nodded again and then shook his head. Decker sighed heavily and leaned back in his chair.

"Wyatt, he wasn't natural so his eyes and his smell were all wrong. He isn't alive like you and me. The man standing there was a…a glamour or some kind of thing. But you can't glamour a smell or the eyes. You can always tell by the eyes."

"What did he say?"

"That's the thing, Wyatt, I can't remember. I remember a fire appeared outta nowhere and we were sitting there listening to him. But I don't know if he really said anything or if he just…thought it and we heard him." Decker shook his head and ran his hand through his long locks.

"That's interesting. Was every meeting like that?" Wyatt was scribbling away in his notepad as he spoke.

"I don't know. I don't remember much about our meeting with The Dark One. Every night Azul would take us out there and every night blended with the next. Before I knew anything was happening…everything changed." He said the last words softly.

"Your sisters found out then, right?"

"Yes. We were…I was confused. They tried to make us stay in the cave one night. They blocked the door and scolded us. Said we were doing things that were bad and that we had to stay inside and away from the dark. I thought then that they were trying to keep us out of the dark of the night. I think they meant a different dark…"

"Sounds like it to me." Wyatt whispered.

"Well, one evening my sisters weren't in the cave. It wasn't yet full night so Azul couldn't go out. Theo was worried about them because that's what Theo does, he worries. I didn't know it then but they were down by the river waiting for Him. I don't know what happened. When the sun went down, we left the cave and found Him there. I remember he was angry. He was angry we hadn't told him about our sisters." He sighed heavily and spun his hat on his finger.

"That's when he said they were dangerous, right?" Decker nodded his head. "When you went back to the cave that morning, were they there?"

"No. They were gone. Theo cried and sulked for ages. Azul flew out every night looking for them but never found them. I tracked them to a nearby field but from there their smell was gone. Vasha, he stayed quiet and mourned in his own way. One night, Azul simply never came back. We waited for him but he left us as well."

"Oh, I bet Theo took that so hard." Wyatt said. Decker smiled a tight, painful smile.

"We all did. He was our eldest brother. Our protector. One morning when I woke up, Vasha was gone too. With him, every piece of jewelry and rug that had made it a home was gone with him. Me and Theo were all that was left."

"Did they leave to find the girls?" Wyatt asked.

"I don't know. I know when I left…I left so I wouldn't be sad anymore."

Chapter Two

"Where did you go, Decker? When you left the cave alone?" Wyatt asked him. Decker searched on the ground for his pack of cigarettes and lit one without saying anything. He blew the smoke out and tilted his head back to see the night sky.

"I just walked. It was easy for me to pass as a regular person. I could move around in the day time as well as the night. I stopped in villages but never stayed too long. Someone always noticed my eyes and then there'd be trouble. They'd make me go, afraid I was a demon or some other nasty, unnatural thing." He laughed to himself and flicked the ashes from his cigarette.

"How long did you do that?" Wyatt asked as he wrote in his notepad. Decker's face took on a pained expression as he mentally calculated the question.

"I wasn't more than twenty years or so at that time." He took another drag from his cigarette and blew small smoke rings into the night sky. "I want a cigar. You like cigars?" He turned and his yellow eyes met Wyatt's hazel ones.

"No. I don't like smoke actually." He gave Decker a small smile and looked back at his notes. "So...where did you go in your wanderings? Did you travel far?"

"Once I decided that the girls...once I knew they were gone for good, I went to the place I'd heard about my whole life. Egypt." Decker's face brightened with a smile and he flashed his razor sharp teeth when he did. "Now that is a lovely place. Well, back then it was. Now it's full of shit stink and those once lovely people don't know their head from their arse anymore. But back then, that was the place to go to feel like you've seen the world."

"Wow. I can't imagine what that was like," Wyatt said in awe.

"Nar...you'd have to have seen it to believe it, Wyatt. The rich folks wore gold on every part of them. Draped in the finest silks with a troupe of slaves to cater to their every whim, the wealthy ones glittered like jewels. I always wondered why Vasha never made it there. Maybe I'll ask him about that someday." He shook his head and waved the thought away. "But the poor, they were very poor. The slaves were better off than the poor folks."

"What did you do there?" Wyatt asked him.

"I decided I'd make a name for myself and earn my keep. I had valuable skills so I thought I should put them to good use. I answered the call of the Rome and enlisted into her army," Decker said with a smile.

"You were a Roman soldier. Unbelievable..." Wyatt shook his head as he rapidly scribbled notes on his paper.

"Oh, yeah. Training was a breeze and I quickly moved up in rank."

"No one ever noticed your...uh..." He gestured to his eyes.

"That's the bloody miracle of all. They did notice and didn't give a damn. I think they thought I was some kinda bloody good omen. Once the others saw it didn't bother the *Primus pilus*, the man in charge of our unit, then they didn't pay me any mind. You see, I said I moved up quickly in ranks and I did. I went from being a common foot soldier to a very specialized group of soldiers called *Immunes*."

"What was your job, then?" Wyatt asked. Decker smirked at Wyatt's innocent question and shook his head. "I told you I put my natural skills to work, Wyatt. What do I do best, pretty boy?" he asked with a smile.

Wyatt looked at Decker and back to his notes and nodded. "Of course, you were some sort of assassin, right?" Decker let out a barking laugh and smacked Wyatt on the shoulder.

"That's right. I remember the first time I stepped foot on the sands for recruits to practice on. We wore brown wraps, the color of a new recruit. I was bigger and stronger than every single one of them. The blokes training us up were pleased I could draw blood so quickly with a sword. You see, many of the soldiers were young and hadn't the muscles to wield a sword the way I could. The wooden practice swords were child's play to me."

"Hey...You're teaching Mela with a wooden sword. Are you training her like you were trained back then?" Wyatt asked.

"Nope. I'm training her better than I was. I've got much more experience now than they ever did when they taught me. But..." he tossed his cigarette into the yard and picked up his hat. "Back then, they were the best. Plus, I had friends, slept in a tent, and ate food every day. It was a good life," he concluded with a nod of his head.

"After you finished training, what then?"

"Ah...well, that was when they put my special skills to work every now and again. I only had one request: I didn't want to be on no ships. Those fuckers sank all the time. Easy prey and I didn't know how to swim," He shook his head vigorously. "I was having none of those damned warships. My brother-in- arms, Claudius was his name, we were paired together and had a lot of fun. We drank a lot and we whored around...you know what I mean?" He wiggled his eyebrows at Wyatt and they both laughed.

"Yes, Decker, I know what you mean." Decker laughed even harder and clapped a hand on Wyatt's back.

"No, you don't, brother!" They both laughed harder and it took them a few minutes to calm down. Decker placed his hat on his head and settled back in his chair. "Those were good times."

"So….this was near Alexandria, yes? I read about this in school. I know it's not the same thing," he said quickly. "But I'm familiar with history."

"Aye, near Alexandria. They wanted to be near their blasted ships. It was Hannibal they were fighting with then. Hannibal…what a man." He shook his head in admiration.

"You admired him even though you fought against him?"

"Oh yes. The Carthaginians knew the arts of war. They weren't the best I've seen but, for shit's sake, they caused Rome an awful lot of trouble. In one of their sea battles, they asked for extra men to come aboard. I had an arrangement with my *Legionaries* but Claudius didn't. He was gone over two weeks before I got the news he'd drowned for the glory of Rome off the coast of some damn island." He looked down and pursed his lips for a moment. Wyatt stayed silent.

The sounds of the night echoed around them and the fire crackled in the pit. Wyatt stood, stretched his legs, and went over to the fire. He took his time placing another log in the flames and knelt down to watch it catch. After a few moments, Decker came and knelt beside him.

"I'm sorry about your friend," Wyatt said softly.

"Ah…it was so long ago…doesn't matter no more," he said as he looked deeply into the fire.

"In any case, I'm sorry." Wyatt extended his hand and patted Decker's shoulder. Decker frowned slightly but said nothing more. Wyatt stood and brushed the dirt from his pants.

"You wanna know more? Or is this enough?" Decker asked him.

"Oh, I want to know more. Lots more. When you're ready though." Wyatt smiled as Decker stood and followed him back to their chairs. "We left off with the warships and all that while you were in Egypt. How long did you stay there?"

"Let's see…I stayed for a long time. Then it was time for me to transfer somewhere else, you see. I didn't age like the others and by this time I'd been in the army almost twenty years." Wyatt's eyebrows raised and he continued to scribble notes as Decker spoke. "I left on a transport ship for Rome about…well…I'm not sure what year it would've been." He cocked his head to the side and strained to recount his long history.

"You finally got on a ship?" Wyatt asked, tapping his pencil on the paper.

"Oh yeah…If I wanted to leave Egypt, that was the quickest course. I needed to get to Rome to fill my new orders. I think I was piss drunk the entire trip. I can't tell you how happy I was when the shout came that we were approaching land. When I was back in Rome, I happened to run across my eldest brother one night."

"Seriously? Azul was in Rome?"

"Well, picking off cattle or vagabonds off the road to eat, I don't know. I was attached to a patrol unit in Rome since they had no real need for assassins inside Rome herself. Yet." He pointed his cigarette at Wyatt. "I went out, looked up, and caught a glimpse of something in the sky. My eyesight is much keener than a regular human's." He proudly tapped his forehead and nodded at Wyatt.

"Did he see you?" Wyatt asked.

"I didn't think so at first. However, as we rode our horses back to the city gates, all of a sudden I heard a very loud voice scream, and I knew it was him. He'd smelled me. I told the boys I was with to ride hard for the gates. We tried to outrun him. But there's no outrunning Azul once he smells you. Like a damn bullet he flies and let loose fire at us."

"Fire? How'd he do that?" Wyatt asked confused. Decker took another drag from his cigarette and eyed Wyatt.

"You ain't figured it out yet, Wyatt? My eldest brother is what your lot calls a dragon. He breathes pure fire. Scales and a tail and large sharp teeth. Just like the stories tell it."

"No shit. Does Mela know this?" Wyatt was alarmed and couldn't help but look up into the sky searching for something. Decker laughed and patted his knee.

"He ain't here, Wyatt. I've learned a trick or two since that day."

"What happened? Why did he try to burn you? What happened to the other men you were with?" Decker waved his hands at Wyatt to make him stop talking.

"One question at a damn time. First off, I don't know why my brother does what he does. He's cold inside, not like me and all my warm glory." He smiled and tipped his hat at Wyatt. "I think he was dead inside even then. He recognized my scent and wanted me dead. Me and boys escaped his fires, but he took out a large corner of town in the process. I remember folks were worried about the Temple of Vesta. The damn temple housed fire! Why, for Jupiter's sake, were they worried about the damn building burning down when it already had fire inside it?" They both laughed.

"No one asked where the fire came from?"

"Everyone just assumed it was Hannibal's men up to no good, and I felt it was fine if they thought that. No sense in telling them the truth."

"I agree."

"Well, that night led up to some interesting events. Folks much higher up than myself decided to exact revenge for the imagined slight. I, and a few others, were sent behind enemy lines to capture prisoners of worth. You know what that means, dontcha? Fancy Senator's sons in shiny armor. They were easy to spot and even easier to capture." Decker chuckled as his memories played like a blurry movie, slowly becoming clearer.

"How long did you stay a Roman soldier?" Wyatt asked him. Decker shrugged his shoulders and took another drag from his cigarette.

"I know I left when the damned Gauls invaded. What a mess, Hannibal on one hand and stinking Gauls on another. The Senators, with their pure white robes and perfumed asses decided to stop feeding the foot soldiers but one meal a day. There's no honor in treating your men like dogs. More than a few of us went to greener pastures, as they say."

"Where were greener pastures then? I mean, if everyone was fighting with each other, that is." Wyatt stopped writing and looked at Decker's profile in the firelight.

"We sided with a man of whom we knew much. He had the respect of his men and a fierce fighting force. Can you guess, smarty pants?" Decker looked at Wyatt and smiled slyly. Wyatt frowned and tapped his lips with his pencil. "Give up? Hannibal. We crossed over and fought for Hannibal."

"No way!" Wyatt smacked Decker with his papers. "You turncoat!"

"That was the times. I'd done all I could do in the service of Rome and, let's face it, Hannibal's men were having more fun. They won battles and were rewarded for their efforts. I ended up fighting the perfumed Romans!" Decker slapped his knee with his hat and laughed merrily at the memory.

"You are something else." Wyatt made some notes and let Decker regain his composure. "Hey…didn't Hannibal attack Rome herself at one point? I can vaguely remember…" Wyatt scratched his head and searched his memories of history class. Decker nodded.

"Too right you are. We marched straight into Rome, fucked her up the ass, and would have taken her too. The damned weather stopped us. Can you believe it? Militaries now days aren't stopped by a fuck-all thing like the weather. The damn storm threatened to drown us all and we were forced to retreat. Pity."

"Imagine, had you not retreated, what would've happened?" Wyatt wondered out loud.

"Hell if I know. Oh," Decker snapped his fingers and turned to Wyatt. "I do remember some big hullabaloo over an ancient stone. What was the name?" He smacked his feet in frustration with his hat as he thought.

"Tell me about the stone then, if you can't remember the names, maybe I can," Wyatt offered.

"There was an ancient Goddess, some Mother of something, and there was a stone they said was from the Heavens…Anyway, I remember folks from everywhere wanted it and Rome had it. Of course. But the stone was said to have powers and…*Idaean* maybe? Not sure. But I was part of a small group of mercenaries who were told to attempt a thievery of it. Special magical powers or visions of the future were supposed to come to the one who holds it. I don't remember the whole story right now…"

"That's okay. I'll see what I can look up and find out. That'll be interesting. Were you able to steal it? The magic stone?" Wyatt asked.

'Nar…Before we could execute those orders, the honorable Hannibal and company was needed in Africa. Damned shame. I think a bit of stealthy thievery would have been fun. Plus, if the rumors about the stone were true, maybe things would have turned out different for him."

"What happened to him? I forget."

"Found himself surrounded and stuck a sword in his gut instead of being taken. Good way to go, I think. That kind of death is preferable to a real soldier instead of being someone's trophy. A death in battle is the better of the two, but there it is. He would've been carted about and made to endure shame and suffering, not given a clean death. We weren't there at the time, my men and I. Many of us stayed in Alexandria trying to recruit more soldiers. Damn shame." Decker lit another cigarette and studied a spider that was crawling up his pant legs. He watched it slowly struggle to climb higher with an amused smile.

"It's getting late, Decker. You think we could call it a night?" Wyatt yawned and stretched his arms over his head. Decker nodded and stood up.

"Sure thing. If you want to know more, I got more to tell."

Wyatt smiled. "I'm sure you do. You can bet your ass I want to hear more. But I need my beauty sleep." He placed a hand on Decker's shoulder. Decker put his hand on Wyatt's shoulder and smiled his toothy grin.

"You know, this is how friends greeted one another back then."

"Are we friends, Decker?" Wyatt's face lit up. Decker shrugged his shoulders and nodded slightly. Wyatt closed the distance between them and embraced Decker with gusto. Decker fought to pry himself from his grasp.

"Get off. That's enough of that."

Wyatt laughed, waved and wished him a goodnight as he opened the backdoor to go inside. Decker waved at him over his shoulder and stepped off the porch in to the darkness.

Chapter Three

Decker watched Mela as she went inside for the night. It was another late night of training and she'd done well. He smiled and thought he made a wonderful teacher if he could have her fighting like that in such a short time. He worried for her though. He watched Mela through the windows, still innocent in the eyes of a warrior, as she made her way through the house. She hadn't taken a life yet, and until she did, she would be at a disadvantage from the part of her that mourns and feels guilt. He worried she wouldn't be willing to and that was the thought that kept him up at night. She needed to be a killer.

She would hesitate--he could feel it. She wasn't ready to face a real life or death fight, not yet. Until she was truly ready, he'd keep watch at night. Until he knew, without a doubt, that she would use her sword as if it were a part of her, and with no thought of the outcome, he would worry. He wondered if Wyatt would come now that the day's training was done. Telling him stories from the past brought up many memories, and a deep longing he hadn't known was there began to bother him.

Decker sat in his chair. It was his because he told everyone it was, and for now he rested his feet on the porch railing. Despite what he previously thought, he felt comfortable here at Mela's home, and with his brothers. His affection for the girl was deepening every day, much to his surprise. When she moved with graceful purpose, he was so proud of her accomplishments. When she couldn't manage to do something quick enough to suit her, he wanted to help her more. Yes, he knew he had become very fond of Mela. She was kind, but mouthy too. He liked that. She didn't scold him often for being uncouth and she laughed at his jokes. It was almost like...

"Hey there, Decker!" Wyatt's voice broke into his thoughts and Decker nodded his greeting to him. Wyatt was such a pretty man, Decker thought. He would've done well back in a time when a man's beauty was considered just as important as a woman's. He smelled nice too, just like a proper Roman.

"Evening, Wyatt. What brings you out on a crisp, dark night?" Wyatt didn't respond as he sat in the chair beside Decker and handed him a box.

"For you. I hope you like it." Wyatt said, flashing his brilliant smile. Decker eyed him for a moment and opened the lid to the box.

"Ohhh…" Decker couldn't help but smile. Wyatt had given him a box of cigars. He lifted one of the brown cylinders and held it up to his nose. He closed his eyes and breathed in the thick, heady aroma. "Lovely." Completely chuffed at his gift, Decker swiftly bit the tip off of the cigar and lit the other end. He puffed on it for a while to let it catch fully and the thick blanket of musky smoke covered the back porch.

"Good?" Wyatt asked with a hint of laughter in his voice.

"Oh yeah. Thanks, pal." He smacked Wyatt on the back once and sat back in his chair, completely relaxed. Wyatt watched him for a moment, pleased with the look of happiness on Decker's face. The genuine pleasure he saw in Decker's smile made the difficult task of buying a box of good cigars worth it.

"Right…So, are you ready to talk some more?" Wyatt asked him, already pulling out his pad of paper and recorder. Decker smiled and nodded his head as he tried to remember how to blow smoke rings.

"And what, may I ask, is going on?" Vasha's sultry voice tickled the air. Both men looked to see Vasha walking towards them from the shadows. Each step he took was full of seductive grace. All four of his arms extended out to touch the trees as he passed them. With his silent approach, he brought an overwhelming mixture of fragrances. Vasha spent much of his time bathing himself with perfumed soaps, rubbing perfumed oils into his blue skin, or smoking an assortment of pungent herbs from his Hookah. "It looks like a party and I want to know why I wasn't invited."

"Bugger off, Vasha. Wyatt here is interviewing me, ain't ya? He wants to know all about my life, and all the stuff I've done." Decker sounded slightly whiney and Wyatt smiled.

"Yes. Decker has an amazing history and I wanted to hear every detail and write it all down." Wyatt said as he patted Decker's shoulder. Vasha held Wyatt's gaze for an instant and smiled. He looked away and nodded his head.

"Very well...I'm well aware my dear brother has had an exciting existence. Far be it from me to interrupt. Tell me, brother, will you allow me to hear your stories as well one day? I too am curious about a few things." Vasha's deep, throaty voice carried in the night.

"Aye. But Wyatt asked first. He's got dibs," Decker said, jabbing his finger in the air at Vasha.

"Very well, my darling brother." He bowed slightly from the waist and for a moment his long back was exposed from the top of his head all the way to the end of his tail. "I shall leave you. But Wyatt," he leaned in and his piercing yellow eyes locked onto Wyatt's, "I expect you to have a few questions for me one day, yes?"

"Yes, you know I do." Wyatt winked at Vasha who turned and sauntered off into the shadows once more.

"He's something else," Wyatt said to himself. "Okie dokie, Decker, we left off...let's see...Oh, right. Hannibal was dead and you were in Alexandria still."

"Yeah...Hannibal dead. I was thinking about something you might be interested in. Oy, have you ever heard of the Sibylline Books?" Wyatt frowned and shook his head. His paper and pen at the ready, he scribbled the name down on paper. "The Sibylline Books were a big deal in, what you'd call, ancient times. Oh aye…many King, Emperor, and General wanted their hands on those books. Folks said they could tell the future. Not sure who wrote 'em. But they would be consulted in difficult times."

"Like an Oracle?" Wyatt asked. Decker puffed on his cigar and shook his head slightly.

"Nah…there's a subtle difference between the two, you see. Oracles were answers to questions asked. These Sibylline Books, they were written…garsh…hundreds of years before I was born. That outta tell you something." He nodded his head at Wyatt.

"Did you ever see them? The books?" Wyatt asked with unmasked awe in his voice.

"Let me tell you this here little story. I was thinking after you went off to bed last night about what came after my time in Rome's Army. Then I remembered the tale…" Decker leaned forward with his elbows on his knees and told the story of the Sibylline Books to Wyatt as he watched the memories play in his mind like an old movie.

"This happened right after the Romans burned Carthage. See, everything was topsy turvey for a while and I didn't quite know where I was gonna land. I packed my belongings and caught a ship back to Rome. There, I was known to the, let's just say, the unsavory sorts," He winked at Wyatt who knew of just the sort he was referring to. "Aye, I made my living as only I knew how. It's amazing how much coin a well-to-do Senator or Praetor will pay to rid themselves of annoying adversaries. Or an unnecessary burden of a wife."

"Decker…you killed innocent women?"

"Only a few. But innocent they were not. Be sure of that. My point is this…I was the one the rich men came to when they needed something done from the shadows. I had no family ties so I couldn't be connected to their secrets and lies. It so happens on this one day, a man by the name of Cornelius Antionius wanted my services. He had other names mixed in there, but he was a well known Senator of the times. He was a twat. And coming from me, that's saying something."

"Damn…." Wyatt shook his head and wrote the name down.

"The man was horrid, Wyatt. He was a thief, a scoundrel, a murderer, a liar and even worse than all that… he was a cheat in the games. All of them. If it involved money, he was in on it."

"You don't say."

"I do. He sent his henchmen to fetch me one night. I had a small, humble little place right next to my favorite tavern. I drank and played with women all I wanted back then. Most of the whores either didn't care about my eyes or were too stupid to notice. As long as the shiny coins were placed promptly in their greedy little hands, they'd call me Emperor if I asked them to."

"That's so bad, Decker," Wyatt said, stifling a laugh.

"Aye, but so true. So, this one night, his men came into the tavern asking for me. Back then, I was Dektrios Cannibalius. I gave myself that name. Pretty funny, eh?"

"Hilarious."

"I thought so. There were three or four, I don't remember really. But they wore the armor of their master and tossed bags of coins in the air and caught them in their hands. The jingle jingle of coin brought all the whores. All it took was a few of them and those little bitches brought the men right up to my room."

"Never trust a ho', Decker." Wyatt said, laughing.

"Ain't that the truth. I opened my door and what do I see? They tell me they came to bring me to their master, Cornelius, and that I had to come right away. They tossed a bag of coins at my feet. I remember thinking I should go ahead and kill them then, but I thought better of it. Too many eyes and too many ears. I obviously couldn't trust the patrons of the establishment."

"Obviously."

"Right. So I scooped up the coins from the wooden floor and the one in front, as I turned my back on them to count the coins, kicked me in the back. I fell into the table, broke a vat of wine, and spilled the coins everywhere. They went rolling around on the wooden floor. 'Hurry up,' they called to me. Wyatt, I was ready to kill them. I wanted to and I knew I would. But curiosity got the better of me. I grabbed my sword and cloak and followed like a good little dog."

"I can't believe you had that much restraint."

"Me neither, Wyatt. Me neither. But those times were harsh and I had no real friends left. No army I belonged to. Except the whores. The army of whores were mine, I guess." He laughed at his own joke. "But a fat load of horse shit they were good for. We made our way to the honorable Cornelius Antionius's villa. Slaves lined the walls in this place. He even kept gladiators, I'm told, but they were kept out of the city. He was seated behind a large table with all sorts of papers laying about, placed there to make him look important, no doubt."

"Some things never change, huh?"

"Aye. So, as I stand there, the soldiers who came to fetch me stood on either side of me. Cornelius shuffled papers around, looking busy and important, and then motioned for his slave to fill his wine cup."

"Were there a lot of slaves in Rome?"

"Yeah. They were everywhere. People stolen as spoils of war, kidnapped, most of 'em were. They spent their lives in servitude to men like Cornelius. Pouring his wine, wiping his ass, and fucking everything they were told to fuck for either amusement or pleasure. Sometimes...it was for pain. I found that was the case with the honorable Cornelius. But I'll get to that part..."

"He sounds like a real asshole," Wyatt said, frowning.

"He welcomes me into his home and offers me a glass of wine. 'Drink, show me honor by sharing a cup of wine.' That's how he spoke. To refuse such a thing would have insulted him greatly."

"You shared wine with that asshole?"

"Nope. I refused. I said my back hurt too much after getting kicked around by his little soldiers." Wyatt and Decker both laughed. "He stood there, with the cup of wine extended out like this," Decker held his arm out in front of him. "And he just blinked a few times. I didn't take it and everything got real quiet. Then, he just smiled and took a drink himself. Then he said, 'Well, Dektrios Cannibalius, I've heard rumor that you're the man to come to if one needs something…difficult done.' He looked real uncomfortable after that. You know why? He saw my eyes. It was the first time he'd bothered to look me in the eye. I could tell he was afraid. I could sense his fear like a cornered rabbit. So, I decided to go in for the kill."

"You killed him right there?" Wyatt screeched.

"Shush…I smiled at him. There's no surer way of scaring someone than to smile at them. Showed my teeth, that is. He stammered and then he couldn't look at me no longer. He sat back down behind his big table and slid a piece of parchment to me."

"What did it say?" Decker shrugged.

"Hell, I don't know. I didn't reach for it. I simply stood there and waited to see what he would do. After a few minutes went by, everyone shifting about all nervous like, he told me what he wanted. There was a man who had some sensitive information about him and he wanted that man gone. I asked him, I said real quiet like, 'You want me to kill this man?' He nodded his head, gestured to the damn paper again, and said that was a promissory note for a whole lot of money. It was mine if the man died."

"What a pleasant man," Wyatt said.

"I asked who it was that needed to die and he told me...I forget his name now. But I agreed and the honorable Cornelius told me to come back with proof of the man's death." Decker smiled.

"Oh no...you didn't, did you?"

"Aye, I brought him the man's head." Decker said, laughing.

"You did! Oh, you're disgusting." Wyatt knew it was Decker's way but his desire to lob off body parts turned his stomach.

"When I returned with the proof, Cornelius was in one of his bedrooms...real fancy. Silk hung from the doorways and pillows lay scattered all about. It was the kind of place Vasha would love. He was there with one of his slaves. He had her tied up like one would tie a sow for slaughter. Her feet and hands were bound together and she was gagged. But I could see she was bleeding..."

"That's horrible..." Wyatt covered his mouth with his hand.

"It was horrible. What he did to that girl was his way of...you know...gettin' his jollys. He was nude and he was...er...real excited. The things he did to that young girl...terrible. You know the worst part? The worst part was when he turned and saw me. He simply greeted me like an old friend and invited me to join him. He asked, 'Did you bring me something, Dektrios?' Did I ever. From a bag, I pulled out his enemy's head and tossed it at his feet."

"Gross, but poetic."

"Thanks. I thought so too. He bent over and picked up the head and held it like he was gonna kiss it. I realized then how deep the sickness had hold of that man. As he fondled the dripping head, and touched it with entirely too much excitement than I wanted to witness, I checked on the girl. She was bleeding from her girl parts and from her breasts. He'd cut one of them clear off. I touched her cheek where I saw a tear and she opened her eyes."

"Oh, good God."

"No God there that night for her. Her eyes…I still remember them. They were blue. She was a slave from Germania. Real pretty thing. She had long blonde hair but it was chopped off in places too. When she looked at me, fear was there. I could feel her begging me to help her too. I made my decision right then and made a plan."

"Please tell me you killed him. Seriously, tell me," Wyatt demanded.

"I stepped out of the room. Cornelius didn't even notice. I think he was doing something real gross to the head. I saw the guards in the hall and beckoned to them. Slowly, they walked towards me and I took them down in two easy strokes."

"Yes!" Wyatt made a fist and punched the air.

"I turned back around and entered the room again. Cornelius had his naked back to me and I pulled my sword on him. "I want payment, Cornelius.' I said to him. He didn't even seem to notice me at first. I poked his back with my sword and he slowly turned around. "Yes, yes, of course. It is in my office…let me call someone to get it for you.' I was a little worried about more guards but he rang a bell and another frightened girl answered from another doorway. He sent her scurrying off for my money and we were alone again. Me, the bleeding girl, and the naked man with the severed head."

"Hurry…tell me what happened. I can't stand it." Wyatt wasn't taking notes anymore. He was leaned all the way forward, wringing his hands.

"The girl came back with the rolled up parchment and handed it to her Master. He handed it to me. All the while, he was staring at the head dangling by the hair in his other hand. He'd completely forgotten about the girl he'd been hurting too. I grabbed the paper from him, unrolled it, and read the large amount of money owed to me. It was a lot of gold. Enough where I could live in luxury for a long time. He'd really wanted that man dead. He turned his back to me and went to the girl. He pet her head like she was a dog. She was bleeding a lot, I was sure she was done for. I didn't want her to die tied up like that. That's when I hit him real hard in the back of the head."

"Finally!"

"He was out of it. The head he held rolled outta his hands and his naked, fat body looked like a beached whale on the floor. I worked on untying the girl first. I had to be real careful because when she moved, she bled more. I told her I'd find her a *Medicus*, that's what would be one of your doctors, but she shook her head. 'I die,' she told me. It was true. She was bleeding from a bunch of places, and in such large amounts, there weren't nothing anyone could do for her. I sat on the marble floor with her in my lap like a wee child. I was covered in her blood and she smiled at me. It was the damndest thing, Wyatt. The girl was dying, in a lot of pain, but she smiled and held my hand."

"She was thankful for you, Decker. You tried…"

"Aye. But she died. I watched her go real quiet like. I don't mind fighting 'til the death. Blood and battle are both good ways to go. But her death was sad…so sad. I set her down on the ground and focused my attention on Cornelius, who was starting to wake up. Do you really want to know what I did to him?" Decker searched Wyatt's face for approval.

"Oh yes. I want to know exactly what happened to him."

"I tied him up like he did the girl. I cut him as he did the girl. I removed his manly bits as he screamed and choked on the gag. I waited until he bled out, then I cut off his head."

"Good for you. I can't believe I just said that." Wyatt put his head in his hands. "It's just awful."

"Aye. It was. It was a good night for me because I was a wealthy man of means after that. Of course, I had to move out from my comfy room next to the tavern and say goodbye to my army of whores." Decker and Wyatt both laughed.

"Where did you go?"

"Not too far away. I adopted another name, Dektrios Liberatero. It had a nice ring to it. I bought me a house and had servants of my own. But I didn't mistreat mine the way he did, no sir. I was a fair master and they were good to me. It was while I lived in that small villa, I met a man by the name of Benidito Mercado. He was an eccentric man and he liked to drink. A lot. We'd spend night drinking and fooling around with loose women…those were good days. But one day, Benidito brought another man to visit my villa. This man was from Africa. He was trying to put together a group of men who would help him find something very rare and very powerful."

"What was he looking for?"

"Oy, you got a short memory. The Sibylline Books. I got it outta Benidito when the African man was in the garden. He said the man would pay handsomely for any assistance and he had other powerful friends that were already in the cue to help him. You got to understand, this was something of legend back in those days. Many people in unsavory circles were searching for it. Some were looking for it for money, some were looking for it for power, and some were looking for it because they had a thirst for the divine." Decker laughed. "It was all horse shit. Benidito thirsted for adventure but me, I wanted to enjoy life for a bit longer there in my villa."

"You didn't go with them?"

"Nah…I should've though. My pal Benidito got himself nice and dead because of it. He wouldn't have died if I'd been there. But he was foolish for going. I heard from the two slaves who returned that a monster protected the books. That monster tore them all to bits. I tried to get more information from those damn slaves, but they were too frightened or didn't have the words to explain anymore."

"Okay. So you never saw these books?"

"No. I was able to figure out where they went to find them. Since those books tell the future, I wonder if they got anything in 'em about what's going on now? You think?" Decker looked at Wyatt in question.

Wyatt frowned and chewed on the end of his pencil "I don't know. We'd need to know more about them, what was written in them, and all that. Let me do some research and then we'll maybe bring it up to Mela." Decker nodded his head in agreement and both men sat quietly in the darkness. The fire that constantly burned in the backyard didn't seem to produce as much light as it did before. So much darkness around them all these days. "What did you do after your friend died? You had a nice house and money--what did you do?"

"Aye, I had money and a house. I did what I'd always done. I killed would-be kings, would-be usurpers, I killed arrogant men who lusted for too much power, and I killed them all for money. It wasn't fun but I am what I am."

"That's not all you are, Decker. I don't believe that at all."

"You're a right pal for saying that. I don't know how long I went on that way. Years, I think. I remember when the third war was over between Carthage and Rome though. Carthage burned to the ground. One day they were there, causing trouble, not as they did before, mind you, but still causing trouble for Rome. The next day...nothing but ash."

"Do you know what happened?"

"I got me a few ideas. I was convinced it was Azul for a long time. Not sure about it now, but back then, I was certain he'd come hunting me and burned everything when he couldn't find me. I don't know if it was really that way…"

"Are we going to have problems like this with Azul again? Do we need to prepare for everything to go straight to hell if he decides to come sniffing around here? I mean, you guys found Mela easy enough. Right?" Decker could see the thought terrified him.

"I can hide our scents. I can't do nothing about the magick though. When Mela and the Angel did their little bit of magick, searching for my sisters, it was like a scream in a quiet room. I knew the moment she cast the spell. Someone was meddling, I thought. You see, it wasn't the first time an Elementai cast that spell. I knew what was happening. It had been a long time, but I knew."

"Wait…another Elementai searched for your sisters? Why? I'm kind of fuzzy on the 'why' of all of this." Wyatt frowned.

Decker searched Wyatt's face briefly and shook his head. The others hadn't thought it was necessary to tell Wyatt everything, apparently. Secrets. Too many secrets, that's what Theo always said. It seemed as though he was right. This particular secret could get Wyatt killed and Decker didn't want that. "I mean," Wyatt continued, "I think it's great Mela is trying to help you guys reunite but if that means bringing dragon-brother around…I don't know."

"Mate, you're a smart man so I won't bullshit you. Mela and the Angel did that spell for a purpose. They need to find my sisters, not for my brothers and me, but for a bigger reason. My sisters got magick all their own. They need that magick." Decker watched as the full purpose to their seemingly unplanned association hit home.

"Oh, my God. She didn't tell me…" Decker waved off his words and placed a hand on his shoulder. He could feel Wyatt's anger rolling off of him.

"Now Wyatt, you have a place with Mela in her natural, normal world. We got a place with Mela in her magickal one. So far, we've been able to mix the two with little trouble. She's kept some of these facts from you in order to protect you. And, to protect herself, I think. She's got to fight them all, pal. The Dark One and his armies, they're preparing for war."

"How can she fight them? Mela doesn't have an army. She's just…Mela." Wyatt said softly.

"Now that, we'll discuss later. But for now, she's got me and my brothers."

"And me! I'm pretty good at doing stuff." Decker shook his head and squeezed Wyatt's shoulder.

"No, Mate. You ain't no fighter. You're soft. No, you need to hear this," Decker saw he was about to be interrupted. "Everyone has a purpose. Mela and I have ours, there's little either of us can do about that. But you got your own purpose, Wyatt. You're her friend and you'll be needed in the future, I'm sure of it. But not for fighting. What you need to do is listen and watch. You know her better than anyone else does. You'll know when she needs you and you'll know what she needs. Besides," he released Wyatt's shoulder. "I'll need your help with a few things here soon enough too."

"Oh?"

Decker smiled at Wyatt. "I said soon. Not now." Wyatt nodded his head in acceptance but said nothing for a long time. Decker let the young man work out his frustration and deal with the pain of ineptitude. Wyatt was struggling with the innate need of a man to protect what he loved, and the knowledge that he couldn't do that. It was a brutal blow. Eventually, he'd come to accept his lot but he'd find other ways to be useful. Decker knew that much about him.

"Why didn't she just tell me everything?" Wyatt finally asked. Decker sighed heavily and turned to face his friend. He saw the pain and disappointment on Wyatt's face.

"If she told you everything, the whole story, what would you've said? Would you have calmed all her fears? Because she's scared shitless, Wyatt. She's terrified of failing. She's terrified of losing folks close to her. You mostly. She's terrified of her powers. She's terrified of all the things that are lurking just out of sight because she's the one that has to defend everyone from those things. Oh, and she's scared she's not normal anymore. Which she isn't. And she tries too hard to keep that boyfriend of hers. That can't last very long."

"How do you know all of this? And what do you mean Mela and Todd won't last very long? They're amazing together." Wyatt turned to face Decker as he spoke. The pain and disappointment from earlier had now turned into anger. That was good.

"How do I know? I know because I know what goes through the mind of a warrior. I know that our deaths mean nothing if it means protecting the lives of those we love. I know a thing or two about being scared of powers I can't understand. I had many a year to let that become a certain and permanent fear. And I know a thing or two about trying to love someone…" Anger and pain filled him even as he fought against it. It was so long ago, how could it hurt this badly still? Why did he think of her now? Damn Wyatt for making him say it.

"Wait, Decker….what do you mean?" Wyatt's entire demeanor changed to one of concern as his anger melted away. Decker stood and backed away from his friend, shaking his head. He wouldn't tell that story. Not that one. No good would come from picking that scab.

She was dead now. She'd been dead a very long time and it was his fault she'd died.

"I can't, Wyatt. I won't." He reached for his hat, now lying on the ground, brushing the dirt off of it. The hat held memories for him as well…but he wouldn't revisit those right now either.

Wyatt stood and grasped his arm. "I'm sorry. I didn't mean to," he said.

Decker gently removed Wyatt's hand and placed his hand gently on his friend's shoulder. It wasn't in this one's nature to be cruel. He hadn't meant to inflict such pain. He reached behind Wyatt's head and pulled him close so that their foreheads touched.

"I know, mate. I know. But some things…some things are better left to fade away. Let it be. I beg you." He hadn't meant to sound as desperate as he did but it seemed to have hit its mark with Wyatt. That's what he needed at the moment, to try and forget again, and to not talk about it. Wyatt nodded and placed his hand on Decker's shoulder, they stood quietly together, eyes locked while the light from the fire danced around in the night.

After a few moments, Decker nodded and turned to leave. There wasn't anything left to say really. Wyatt had heard enough for one night and Decker had said enough for two lifetimes. As he walked farther from the house, the dark of the night surrounded him. He turned to see the fire merrily burning away and allowed himself a moment to remember what he lost so long ago. Why did he say that to Wyatt? Of course the man would question his words, it was in his nature. But Decker underestimated how deep that wound still was after all this time. The moment her face crept into his mind he'd lost all resolve and wanted nothing more than to flee from her memory, even after all these years.

"Brother." Theo's voice interrupted his thoughts. He should've known Theo would be about.

"I'm all right, brother." Decker knew he wasn't doing a good job of hiding his feelings. He turned to face his brother and gave him a sad smile. There wasn't much use in lying, not to Theo. More importantly, there was no use in lying about how he was feeling at the moment. Theo's steps crunched beneath the brown leaves that covered the ground. His tall, dark form came closer. His black fur made it difficult to see where he stopped, and the night began. His eyes glowed a pale yellow light in the dark, much as Decker's did. Theo stopped when he was inches from his brother and looked down at him.

"You are in pain, my brother." He tilted his head to the side. "Love and longing…these things give you such sorrow." His hoarse voice echoed Decker's own pain. All he could do was nod and blinked furiously at the stinging in his eyes. Theo took a step to place himself beside Decker and wrapped a strong, furry arm around his shoulders. Without saying a word, he led Decker to walk further into the night, keeping his brother close.

Decker didn't want to talk but found Theo's company comforting. Together they walked past the shed where Vasha slept. He'd changed the shed into a much more comfortable place since he'd taken up residence there. Now, the tractor sat behind the building and inside was warm and welcoming. The light from his small fire inside shined through the boards of the building. One whiff of the air and Decker could smell an assortment of incense and smoke that were the smells of their little brother.

Theo led him beyond the smells and deeper into the dark of the night. Clouds obscured the little light of the crescent moon, so they walked on in complete darkness. It made no matter to either of them, since they could see perfectly fine in the dark. They continued on in silence until they reached the trunk of an old oak tree. Theo stopped, placed a hand on the tree, and then murmured something to it.

"This is my favorite tree. It is old and it sees much. Just like us." Theo crouched down and rested his back against the tree and it seemed to Decker, for a moment, that it responded. The tree's leaves rustled and it swayed slightly in response. Theo patted the ground beside him and beckoned Decker to him. Sighing, he sat down and took his hat from his head. He placed it beside him and leaned back against the tree, mimicking his brother.

"I will not ask you to tell me of the things that cause you such pain. That is yours to do with as you please. Although, I know much and more about pain…about love…and I know about death. Far too much about death. Those who are doomed to walk this earth for as long as we do have an intimate understanding of these things. Just as this tree has stood for a long time, it too has seen much of pain and death." Decker turned and looked up at the tree. He'd never understood the conversations Theo had with trees or how he had them.

"What's the point, though? What's the point in living this long, seeing the things we've seen, losing what we have?" Decker blurted the questions out into the darkness.

"Do you truly want to know the answer to that, dear brother?" Decker nodded. He'd asked himself these questions for so long, he simply assumed there was no answer. "The answer is, Dektrios, so that we few who continue to live well beyond a natural life may understand death. We may never experience it. Who knows? We do not get sick. We get hurt, but we are most difficult to kill. Many have tried to kill me."

"Aye, me too."

Theo nodded. "None have succeeded. But we understand death and loss better than average mortals do. We, I think, are here to help them understand it. To accept it and to warn them when necessary."

Decker quietly considered what his brother said. Theo knew little about fighting, wars, and killing, that much was true. But Theo had his own well of knowledge full of information Decker never before considered important. Until now.

"I feel like I'm doing just that for Mela."

Theo nodded his head in agreement. "You are. You're preparing her and watching over her. Your training with her is going to help her be successful. However, I would urge you to include her Familiar in the training soon. He's most anxious to assist." Decker hadn't considered that before and contemplated the possibilities.

"That could work." Decker said. Perhaps he'd underestimated his brother after all.

"He's most insistent about it. What of the conversation with Wyatt tonight?" Decker frowned at his brother in the darkness. "Don't be angry, brother, I felt both of your anger like daggers in my belly. I was concerned."

"It was nothing…he just…I'm not angry at the man. I rather like Wyatt. But telling him stuff from my past, some of those stories I can't tell." Decker knew he needn't explain it further. Theo already understood.

"I know. You did well to tell him what he didn't know. I do not know how Mela will feel about it, but you can't take back your words. Words are funny like that, aren't they? They are such a powerful tool. One can speak and calm a beast, tame a tree, and mend a broken heart."

"I won't discuss it, brother." Decker cut him off. Theo placed a furry hand on his brother's knee and sighed.

"I know this, Dektrios. I know. Perhaps it is not I who needs to hear the story, although, I would listen should you ever wish to tell it. I do think, however, that you should choose someone to hear this tale. If you're trusting young Wyatt with your tales of adventure and slaughter, perhaps he deserves to know the other parts of you too.

Consider what he's doing now, sitting through your long history, and reliving it with you. Do you not think he would be a comfort if you were to revisit the painful memories as well?" Decker pursed his lips and wondered what Wyatt would do if he were to tell him the truth of it all.

"It would make him sad. It would hurt to say her name…to remember her…" He couldn't help the tears that crept from the corners of his eyes. One after another, they silently fell and he did nothing to stop them.

"Yet, he would mourn with you, as would I. I feel love in him whenever he is near. He would understand in ways that I, perhaps, cannot. You would do well to share this tale. Speak of her, let loose the tears, and let your heart be healed. In sharing your pain, you will not only heal but also teach young Wyatt about death and the dangers of knowing one of our kind. He is still so very innocent."

Decker nodded in agreement. That much was true. If anyone needed to hear about the dangers, it was the gentle and kind Wyatt.

"Aye. Perhaps you're right. I wasn't prepared for…to remember her is all. Maybe you're right."

Theo nodded his head and stood up to look at the sky. "I will take to the skies and take your watch tonight. Rest easy, brother. Consider what I have said. I know there is much I do not know of your life. I'll admit I'm a little jealous of Wyatt for knowing more of you than I do. It saddens me we do not know much of each other's lives after our short years together."

"You're right about that. Vasha already asked if Wyatt would let him tell his tales too. Maybe you should be next in line and then we could just let Wyatt write them all down." Decker chuckled and Theo smiled.

"I think that is a very good idea." Theo said and leaped skyward. He extended his wings and silently climbed the air until Decker could no longer see him.

Chapter Four

Decker waited the next night for Wyatt to continue their talks, but he didn't come. He waited until after Mela turned off all of the lights inside and then walked around to the front of the house. Wyatt's car wasn't there. Decker sighed as he went back to the fire and tossed his cigarette in the flames. The smoke he exhaled mixed with smoke from the fire.

Fire. Such a formidable opponent. Mela could call a ball of fire to her hands and throw it as easily as tossing a ball. Once she was at her full strength, he shuddered to think of the devastation she could cause. Fire caused such terrible devastation. He closed his eyes and recalled a memory from long ago, when he was still a small child.

In the memory, Azul towered over him, already the size of a large pickup truck. Decker laughed as his eldest brother spit small balls of fire at trees for entertainment. The hiss of the flames as it flew across the field was loud. When it struck the base of a tree, there was an audible whoosh as it went up in flames. Decker remembered clapping his small hands and Azul's satisfied smirk. To Decker the large, scaly body of his brother was as normal as seeing the sun. He remembered watching Azul's eyes, those yellow catlike eyes, glimmer with glee right before he breathed fire.

That was one of the times his sisters reprimanded Azul. Whenever he'd burned the trees, Theo wailed in terror to his sisters. He was young and couldn't help being so sensitive. Theo pleaded with them to make Azul stop. Decker didn't understand why Theo was so upset, even after Azul was scolded. All he cared about was watching the pretty balls of fire fly and making the funny whooshing noise. Azul hung his large, black head in apparent shame and apologized to Theo.

"My apologies, little brother." His voice was soft as he spoke. "Yet, one brother cries and the other cheers. What am I to do?" Akasma approached Azul, holding Theo's hand. She placed a hand on each of them and met Azul's eyes.

"Perhaps, my naughty brother, you should go find new ways to amuse yourselves." Her smile was gentle as she placed a kiss on the top of Theo's head and then on Decker's. He could still recall the way her smile changed when she wrapped her arms around Azul's large head. The gentleness gave way to sadness when she placed her fair cheek on his. "Behave yourself, Azulathane. You are their protector, not their tormentor."

Decker shook his head free of the memories. He began to regret agreeing to Wyatt's request to share his history. He found himself distracted during the day, organizing his thoughts as they came unwillingly from long ago dark places in his mind.

"Did young Wyatt not come this evening?" Vasha said from behind him. Decker shook his head. "Well then, it appears you are free for the night. Come, come share a smoke with me and tell me a tale of murder. Have you murdered many men, brother?" Decker frowned and turned to face his little brother.

"I've killed plenty of men."

"Good. Then you'll have plenty of stories from which to choose. I'm in the mood for blood. Since life is rather….peaceful here…I'll look to you to sate my blood lust," Vasha's bejeweled body glimmered from the light of the fire. Decker, taking one last look at the dark house, shrugged his shoulders and followed Vasha into the night.

The transformation of the shed astounded Decker. What once housed an older tractor, bits of odds and ends, and dirt, now looked freakishly like a room in a brothel. Pillows lined the floor in every color imaginable. Draped here and there were bits of cloth. They were everywhere and Decker had to push past a red one with fringe as he made his way to the light of a lantern in the middle of the floor.

"Mela said to make myself comfortable and I've done just that. Sit." Vasha tossed him an overstuffed purple pillow with golden embroidery. Decker wrinkled his nose and stuffed the pillow under his rear end when he sat. "There, isn't this nice?" Vasha folded himself onto a pile of pillows and smiled at his brother.

"Got anything to drink?" Decker asked. Vasha reached for his elaborate hookah and smiled slyly at his brother.

"Drink? No, dear brother. No drinking tonight. I've got something else in mind entirely," He busied himself with the long pipes attached to the contraption and Decker watched, fascinated, as all four of Vasha's hands worked to pack in a dark black tobacco. At least, he hoped it was only tobacco.

"What's that you're putting in there? It ain't going to make me all nutty, is it?" Decker asked but received no response other than a smile. Vasha was always the sly one. He was elegant and deadly. Decker knew another killer when he saw one. His brother simply looked more innocent – except his eyes. The eyes will always tell the truth. There was a certain look, a vibe, Decker could feel in another soul who's killed. No longer the prey, they're the predator and their eyes were constantly seeking another.

"Here, you will go first." He handed Decker the metal end of the long tube connected to the contraption.

"Why?"

"Because it is the polite thing to do," He chuckled as he reached for a long match and lit the black tobacco-like leaves. "Go on." Decker narrowed his eyes at his brother and inhaled.

The thick smoke filled his lungs and he held it in as long as he could before releasing it. The aftertaste reminded him licorice and dirt. He licked his lips and took another, deeper, hit from the hookah. His head, already swirling, began to feel light. He stared at the designs on the base of the hookah. Naked women decorated the bulbous base. The artist captured them, painted in purple ink, in various stages of twirling and jumping. He marveled at the naked form of the women. They were drawn sparingly, without too many details, but the clad figure of women rarely needs details. The curves of their hips and voluptuous breasts were all the important parts.

"Are you well, Dektrios?" Vasha asked from far away. He felt the metal pipe fall from his hand and he watched it slide from the pillow and land with a thud on the floor. He slowly raised his eyes and looked at his brother.

"What'd you give me?" He wasn't sure if he said the words out loud, or if he only thought them. His arms were growing heavy and it was almost impossible to hold his head up. He knew Vasha was doing something but he couldn't focus on his brother enough to find out what it was. He couldn't focus on anything. Moments later he heard the unmistakable sound of a drum beat. *Thump. Thump. Thump.*

"Relax, Dektrios. You will not be harmed. Lie back and relax…close your eyes and see what it is you were meant to see. I will be here watching over you." Vasha sounded so far away and the pillows were coming closer to his face. With one final futile attempt to sit up straight, Decker slumped face first into a nest of fluffy pillows. They were so soft and smelled faintly of sweat and perfume. He closed his eyes and gave in.

He could hear his brother humming to himself as he gently tapped the drum. *Thump. Thump. Thump.* Decker could smell the smoke that lingered in the air from the hookah. His body felt as if he were falling and tumbling through space.

He saw images, first foggy and then a bit clearer, come into focus. A battlefield. Men in sparse armor, fighting one another under a bright sun. Thousands of them screamed as they rushed toward their enemies. The sweet sound of swords kissing in battle excited Decker and he watched the battle with interest. The metallic taste of blood tickled his throat when he breathed. One after another, the men fell to the ground. Crimson poured from their wounds and their screams echoed in his head. He watched the blood of the opposing armies run together until it was one pool. Deeper and deeper the blood flowed until it swallowed the battlefield and every man on it.

The blood turned into the sea and Decker was on a ship. He felt the sway of the ocean beneath his feet. He looked around and knew this ship from long ago. Men hurried here and there, hoisting sails, scrubbing the deck and carrying crates of supplies below. The seagulls cried from their perch on the mast while Decker stood and stared.

"You can't be here, lad," a man said. Decker turned and saw the face of a kindly man, weathered by the sun and sea.

"Why not? Where am I?"

"You ain't one of us now, are ya?" The man laughed and turned away from Decker and, to his horror, he saw the back of the man's head was gone. Nothing remained but a red, slippery hole. Chunks of what had been inside him dropped from his tattered shirt, and landed on the deck. A young boy was on his knees scrubbing the deck with a horsehair brush. Decker leaned in and saw the front of the boy's shirt was wet with blood.

"You boy, what is this place?" Decker asked. The boy looked up with dark, sad eyes. Blood bubbled from his mouth when he tried to speak. His mouth opened. Someone had recently removed the boy's tongue. Disgusted, Decker looked away and looked for a way off the ship.

"Lad, I told you…You don't belong here." The kindly man was standing next to Decker and smiled when he spoke.

"How do I leave?" Decker wasn't one to be afraid often. He began to feel the unfamiliar prickle of fear creep up his back. It made him uncomfortable and angry.

"You want to leave the ship?" Decker nodded. The kind man looked sad for a moment and then nodded his head. "If you say so." In one swift movement, he shoved Decker over the rail, plummeting to the water below.

His body screamed in pain when it crashed into the sea. The cold, dark water swallowed him, dragging him deeper until he couldn't tell which was up. He frantically moved his arms and legs, searching around him for any sign of where the surface was. Above his head, a school of fish swam and the light catching on their scales caught his eye. Determined not to drown, Decker swam with all his might to reach them.

From underneath him, he noticed something swimming closer. He stopped reaching for the surface and looked down. A man, or what was left of him, swam awkwardly up to meet Decker. He was missing a leg and bits of his guts floated behind him like deflated balloons.

"Wait for me… It's lonely down here. I don't like it under the water," the man said. Small fish nibbled on his face and twice a larger fish took bites from his arms. Decker, feeling more desperate than ever to get away, shook his head violently and raced for the surface. Just when he felt his lungs would explode, Decker broke through the water, gasping.

He coughed and gagged, his eyes closed. He didn't want to see anymore. Whatever was coming next, he didn't want to see. He reached out and felt with his hands that he was on dry land. Blessed dry land. On all fours he coughed one last time and readied himself to look around.

It was night and he could hear the ocean somewhere close by as the waves kissed the rocks. He knew this land. He knew it very well. His heart squeezed in his chest as the smell of the Irish northland brought back memories. These memories spanned a long, long time. Friends. A new family. A community that accepted him. The woman who loved him.

Decker rose to his feet and brushed off his pants. He could still smell the ocean and taste the blood in the back of his throat. He took deep breathes of the crisp salty air and felt his fear slowly fade. This wasn't a bad place for him. Too many good memories were here. He felt the cool grass beneath his feet and smiled. He knew if he walked down this hill and followed the stream, he would find a safe place. His home.

With every step he took, long forgotten memories bubbled up one after another. Some made him smile, others made him sad, but he still felt safe. He walked until he saw the familiar shape of what was once his home tucked into the hillside that overlooked the valley below. Smiling, his steps quickened and he found himself reaching for the door latch.

When it opened, Decker was met with many voices of those he'd once known. His brothers-in- arms. His friends. His companions. All of them greeted him with a yell and a hearty pat on the back. Someone handed a mug of ale and his friends surrounded him once more with their welcome. Decker sat beside the fire and welcomed the warmth. He closed his eyes and took a sip of the golden brew.

It tasted salty and sweet, acrid, like death. He spit it out, seeing red come from his lips. It was blood, Decker saw, and he set the cup aside, bewildered. He turned around to ask his friends how this happened but he was alone. Terribly and frightfully alone. Everything was as it had been long ago. The table was bare but for a bowl of flowers in the middle. The floor was swept free of dirt and his traveling cloak hung on a wooden peg beside the door. If he closed his eyes, he could remember her standing just there, by the fire, cooking him their dinner with a warm smile on her pretty face.

"Have you washed your hands, Donagh?" he heard her say. He'd gone so long without hearing the sound of her voice that it brought him to his knees. Decker took deep breaths trying to control his pounding heart and shaking hands. He looked down at them, saw they were shaking, and he let out a small laugh. His hands were filthy.

He heard someone approaching but he was too fearful to look up. Her small bare feet came into view. Her milky white skin, that she took great care to keep clean, always smelled like soap root, he remembered.

He still couldn't look up, even as she placed a delicate hand on his head and gently brushed back his disheveled hair. Decker leaned closer, wrapping his arms around her tiny frame. His face buried in her clothes, he breathed in the all too familiar fragrance of her, and released the sob that was squeezing his throat. He held her tightly as she wrapped her arms around him and placed kisses on his head.

"Don't cry, my love. My one and only love. I'm here. I'm always here." Her voice ripped at his heart but he welcomed the pain. It was her voice. The voice of the one who loved him. Despite even his warnings, she'd loved him. "Why do you cry?" Gasping for breath, Decker pressed his forehead against her belly. His hands wandered, feeling the soft curves of her hips. They were good hips, the way a woman should be.

"Because I miss you…" His voice broke as a new flood of tears choked him into silence. He felt her warm hand slide to his face and cup his chin. He squeezed his eyes shut as she lifted his face. She softly wiped the tears from his cheeks and placed a kiss on his lips.

"Open your eyes, Donagh." she said. Decker took a deep breath and finally looked at the woman he loved so long ago. Her blue eyes mirrored the smile on her face. The long, golden hair, that he loved to touch, hung in soft curls well past her shoulders. She pulled him to his feet and wrapped her arms around his waist the way she had always done. Decker kissed the top of her head as she nestled in his large arms, safe and warm, she always said.

"I miss you…" he said again.

"I never left you," she whispered.

"I'm sorry…It was my fault…"

She looked up and cupped his face in her hands. "No, Donagh. No. Stop this. You must stop. Have you forgotten everything? Have you forgotten our happy years together?" Her soulful blue eyes filled with tears.

Decker held her face in his large hands and rubbed the soft skin on her cheeks with his thumbs.

"I haven't forgotten. I remember everything."

"Then speak of me, my brave Donagh. Remember the good we shared. Not all in your past was dipped in blood. We shared a home and there was love here. You had a family. My Da loved you like a son. Remember us." She kissed him softly on the mouth and continued. "I'll love you for all time, Donagh. Not even death can change that."

Decker pulled her close into a deeper kiss. He tried desperately to taste every bit of her he could. He felt her soft body against him and the longing to lay with her again overwhelmed him. Memories of their lovemaking filled him with a need so intense he gasped.

"I want you," he whispered. She giggled playfully and kissed his neck the way she'd always done.

"Say my name, Donagh. I want to hear you say it once more. Tell me that you love me well." She kissed his throat and nibbled on the tender skin where his shoulder met his neck. He sighed in pleasure and smiled.

"I love you, Cliona. My sweet girl, I love you."

"Never forget what we had, Donagh. It's still there, inside of you. All the love." She kissed his lips. "All the joy." She kissed him again.

"I won't forget." He looked into her eyes. Her love was there for him to see in those warm, blue eyes.

"Kiss me, my love," and without hesitation, without question, he kissed her. He felt love in her kiss and remembered the joy of being loved. He held her tight against him and thought of all of the nights they spent together making love, laughing, drinking, and simply sharing silence. That was love. She was his love.

He lifted her from her feet and carried her to the small bed they shared. It was barely large enough for the two of them but they'd slept entangled in each other's arms so closely, they never bothered to make it bigger. He gently placed her small frame onto the bed and kissed her legs, slowly tracing the curve of her calf and behind her knee. She always giggled prettily when he did that and this was no exception. She reached out for him and held him close to her chest as she stroked his hair.

"Close your eyes, love. It's so quiet and good with you here. Do you feel it?" He closed his eyes and relaxed against her. She was so warm, so comfortable, he couldn't imagine ever wanting to move again. She stroked his hair and began to hum a slow song.

The last thing he remembered was hearing her hum before he opened his eyes and was back in Vasha's shed. Sunlight streamed in between the boards on the walls. How long had it been? A heavy weight filled his chest as reality, that cruel necessity of life, came back to him. He blinked and wiped the drool from his mouth on the pillow beneath him.

Slowly, he sat up and cradled his head in his hands. It was all a dream. He hadn't seen the fighting, the ship, the sea, or Cliona. He sat, elbows on his knees while he held his head, and rocked front to back. She'd been with him. He'd felt her body, smelled her sweet scent, and tasted her kiss.

"Dektrios," Vasha whispered. Decker whipped his head around and glared at his brother. "I didn't know, brother. I never would have thought…"

"Never would have thought what, Vasha?" As rage filled him, his hands began to shake. "Never thought I could love someone? Or someone could love me? What right did you have, brother? By what right do you invade my memories…my memory of her…" He choked back a sob. Vasha sat back, much like a cat would, on his hind legs. He held up his hands to placate his brother's anger.

"I didn't know what the visions would show. I only sought to help you remember things…to help you not be so angry," Decker slammed his fist into Vasha's face. Vasha fell to the side, his head hanging, as blood dripped from his lip. "I'm sorry, brother, for all you've suffered." He slowly wiped the blood away and licked the wound. "Who was she?"

"You deserved that." Vasha nodded in agreement. "She's – was--Cliona," Decker said. His rage deteriorated and he sat back down on the pile of pillows.

"You loved her?" Vasha asked softy. Decker met his brother's eyes that were full of guilt and concern.

"Aye. I loved her. Cliona was my wife."

"Oh, I did not know…" Vasha's eyes filled with tears, but Decker ignored them.

"She was my wife and she loved me. She was a good woman. The best. Beautiful too. Never thought I'd love someone…never thought anybody could love me. But she did." Decker felt an overwhelming peace come over him as he said the words.

"But I love you, brother. Don't you know that?" Decker met his brother's eyes, so like his own, and wondered about him. Had Vasha ever loved anyone? Had anyone ever loved him?

"Aye, Vashanu, I know that. And I love you well. Even though you're a right shit for doing what you did." Vasha smiled as the tears slid down his cheeks.

"Thank you, brother."

Decker nodded and left him in the shed. He needed to talk to Mela.

Chapter Five

Decker waited in the house for Mela to come home from work. It was a real inconvenience that she left so often and he'd often urged her to stop doing it. But she said she needed to for money's sake. He'd need to fix that soon as well. A short time later, he heard her car pull in the driveway and paced in the living room as he waited. Bear happily walked alongside him, wagging his tail. Kat raced for the door when he heard Mela come in, arms full of grocery bags.

"Hey, Decker…here….give me a hand, would you?" she said. He emptied her hands of the bags of food as she closed the door behind her and greeted her furry friends. "What are you up to today?" she asked. Decker placed the bags on the counter in the kitchen, and turned to Mela.

"I need you to call Wyatt on your telephone thing. You tell him I want to talk to him. He didn't come last night."

"Yeah, I know. He had work to do. We have jobs, Decker. I'd love to be able to stay home with you guys all day, and I'm sure he would too, but we have to work. Sometimes that means working at night."

"Well, I don't like it. Besides, he should've told me. Should've sent me a message or something. Now, you go ahead and call him. Tell him he needs to be here tonight. Tell him how serious my face is."

"Got it," Mela said as she pushed buttons on her phone. "Serious face. I see it. I'll tell him." Decker nodded and went to the bathroom.

Cliona would've taken serious offense to his appearance these days. He couldn't remember the last time he bathed. Or the last time he brushed his teeth. His hair was a mess and the dirt beneath his nails was black as tar.

She would've been disgusted at what he'd become. He was a better man when he was with her. He'd been as close to normal as he'd ever been before or after her.

"He says he'll be here tonight!" Mela called out from the other room. Decker took one last look at himself in the mirror and shook his head.

"Oy, Mela, you got a spare razor?"

* * * *

It took almost two hours of scrubbing, a soak in Mela's bathtub, and a shower after that to rid himself of the accumulated filth. He washed his hair but the perfumes in Mela's shampoo made him cringe. He hoped no one would notice that. He shaved his face properly and trimmed his unruly hair so it fell nicely across his shoulders. As he looked over his reflection, he knew Cliona would approve. Mela might not when she saw the ring of brown dirt in her bathtub and the pile of hair on the floor. Or, the fact that he had to use her toothbrush. He needed to remember to tell her about that.

His nails he tended using the neat nail cutters he found in Mela's drawer. It took him a few tries but, after he got the hang of it, the result was clean and trimmed nails. His clothes were simply a pair of pants and those were filthy. Tossing his dirty pants over his shoulder, Decker left the bathroom, naked, and went in search of clean clothes. When he reached the kitchen, Mela was busy making a sandwich.

"Hey, put your pants on!" Mela said.

"I just spent a long time getting nice and clean, thank you very much. I don't fancy putting on my dirty pants. I'm trying to find clean ones," he said, trying to hide his laughter. Her embarrassment was endearing.

"I can wash them for you," she held out her hand while looking the opposite direction. "Just find something else to put on while you wait, please."

"I ain't got nothing else. I guess it's fresh air for all my bits!" Decker laughed as he wiggled his hips.

"No way. I'll find you something. Just stay there," Mela walked past Decker without looking at him. She came back a few minutes later, hand over her eyes, and tossed a pair of pants his direction. They were tight and way too short but at least she'd look at him again.

"These are soft," he said moving his rear end around as he felt the cotton move against his skin.

"Good, glad you like them," she laughed. "I sent Wyatt a message to bring you proper clothes. If anyone can help dress you, it's him."

"I don't need help dressing. I needed clean pants and these here are just fine."

"No, they're not, and yes, you do. Wyatt will be here in a little bit. Say," she frowned, "What made you want to finally shower? I mean, I'm not complaining. At all. You look good all cleaned up. I can finally see your face. I like it."

"Thank you. I'm quite partial to it myself. I just thought it was time to." He avoided looking at her for a few minutes and busied himself by digging through the sacks of groceries on the counter. He could feel her eyes on him though, and sighed.

"If you think Wyatt hasn't told me everything that happened, you're wrong. I know you told him about finding your sisters and I also know that you guys had a bit of an argument the other night. Anything else I need to know?" she asked.

"Wyatt needed to know the truth, Mela. I understand why you didn't tell him but secrets are dangerous now. And no, there isn't anything else you need to know. Except that it's time for you to start your training." He helped himself to a box of cookies and a beer.

Mela grumbled something about finishing her sandwich and Decker laughed as he walked out the back door. He opened his beer, got comfortable in his chair, and looked at the sun, low in the sky. It wasn't too hot anymore but the mosquitos were still bad. He shooed them away when they flew too close. Mela and Bear joined him a few minutes later and he had her run through her drills.

To toughen up her feet, he had her do them all barefoot. That was a riot when she first started. She cried and complained about every poke and sticker in her little dainty feet. But now, now she and the dog took off and began to run without much prompting from him. That was good. She was tough. Tougher than he'd thought she'd be and that pleased him to no end. She was good at picking up exercises as well. He watched her move gracefully and with purpose with the wooden sword he'd made for her. Soon, he'd hand her the real thing, the sword he'd given her for her birthday. That would make her happy.

Three beers later, he called it an early night. Soldiers loved to get a reprieve from training for no reason. It kept up morale. She and the dog were tired and, he noticed as she walked past him, in need of a shower.

"Wyatt's here," she said as she went inside to clean up. Decker, thoroughly enjoying the freedom of the comfortable pants Mela gave him, opened another beer and waited for Wyatt.

"Hello, Decker," he heard from the backdoor. Wyatt stood there with a pile of clothes under his arm and a smile on his face. "I brought you clothes...I see what she means. Get in here and change. You look ridiculous in her pajamas." With that, Wyatt went back inside and Decker, beer in hand, followed.

After a few minutes of fussing, and a solemn oath from Mela not to toss his old pants, Decker agreed to wear blue jeans for the first time in his long life. He didn't like them. But the alternatives were atrocious. Some blue material that looked like it has flower patterns on them and a pair of black pants that were entirely too tight.

"I'll wear these until my own pants are clean," he said as he tried to squat but the pants weren't very forgiving. "But I want my own pants back."

"I promise we won't throw them away. Here," Wyatt tossed a shirt to Decker. "Want to try that on." Decker inspected the scratchy shirt and felt the brittle collar. It was gray but when he held it up, it looked like it shined in the light.

"Nope. I'll go without, thank you," he said as he tossed the shirt back to a laughing Wyatt. "I think I prefer Mela's pants better." But Wyatt refused to give him back the comfortable pajama pants and ushered him out the back door. The sun was already behind the trees and night was creeping up on them. Decker busied himself getting the fire going as Wyatt pulled out his papers and recorder.

"Ready when you are, Decker," Wyatt said. Decker walked past Wyatt, holding up a finger telling him one minute, and went inside for one more thing. He returned shortly with a bottle of whiskey and two glasses.

"What's this?" Wyatt asked as Decker poured them a small glass.

"This, my pretty friend, is whiskey. We're drinking together to put the other night behind us," he said. Wyatt took his, clinked the glasses together, and took a drink. Wyatt coughed and gagged as Decker laughed. "Yeah, it's a bit harsh at first," he said.

"A bit," he coughed. "It's disgusting."

"Ah, an acquired taste, I guess. So, where'd we leave off last time?" Decker asked. Wyatt consulted his papers and read through the last page of notes.

"Looks like after Carthage was burned….Oh right, you thought Azul did it," Wyatt said, scratching his nose with the end of his pencil.

"Right yeah…. Oh, I remembered something. Someone did get their hands on those Sibylline Books after all, you know. For Rome though. Or so they said anyhow, but there it is. After that time, all the legends say the books were there. But being a Roman began to bore me. I got bored of the job too, truth be told."

"The job?"

"Killing fat Romans. It weren't no skill involved, if you get my meaning. They just sat there when I came in and then they'd start blubbering. Some would shit themselves, others cried and tried to bribe me with more money. The worst ones, though, the worst ones were the ones who tried to fight me." He shook his head and took another large drink of whiskey. "Sorry excuse for warriors, that lot was."

"What did you do when you got tired of it all?"

"I freed my slaves and sold my house. There were slave revolts starting, pirates attacking from the sea, and all kinds of shit happening in Asia. I think I needed a wee break from it all. I traveled farther north than I ever had. I saw so many different people on that journey. I made my way through the mountain lands and ended up in Gaul."

"That's France, right?"

"Yeah. Nothing special, really. I learned real quick to avoid the Roman soldiers there. They'd taken over the Gauls and the locals were none too happy about it. I had plenty of money but I took to the fields and travelled at night."

"Where were you going?"

"Not sure at that point. But I realized I hadn't been outside the influence of Rome since I was a young man. So, I went in search of the limits to the Roman empire. I heard where they were staging invasions to the land of Celts and that wasn't going very well. Once I found my way through Gaul," he took another deep drink of his whiskey, "I heard about a lot of fighting with the Germanic tribes and went the other way. That, my friend, took me to the goddamn ocean." Decker refilled his glass and offered Wyatt more but he placed his hand over the glass and shook his head.

"That's a long trip."

"Aye. It was months and months of travelling by cart and mule. I walked but I had some precious belongings, you see. I didn't want to start my new life as a pauper." He took a hefty drink from his glass and lit a cigarette. "It took me a bit but I managed to sell the cart and mule, I don't remember for how much, most likely was ripped off, but I managed to buy myself passage on a boat to take me to the Gaelic lands."

"Ireland?"

"That's the place. They traded with Rome and made friends of them instead of letting themselves get swallowed up into the belly of the beast, so to speak. I admired that, so I set out to see what sort of people they were. I thought I'd meet some mighty warriors, but no. They were tough, no doubt, but they were mostly farmers. Simple folk. But real proud. They knew me right off as a foreigner. I knew I needed to blend in better. Hell, I couldn't understand a damn one of them for the longest time!" Decker laughed and took a long drag from his cigarette.

"Where's your cigars? Don't you like them?" Wyatt asked.

"I like 'em just fine. But tonight I plan on getting drunk, and when I'm drunk, I need cigarettes," he said, bouncing his knee up and down.

"I didn't know we were getting drunk," Wyatt said.

"I didn't say we, I said 'I.' I plan on getting drunk." He swallowed the entire glass of whiskey. "Ain't gonna tell you why neither. You'll see. Just listen and keep writing away," Decker poured another glass, slopping the glass over.

"Now it's important to know that that there weren't nothing special about the Gaelic lands at that time. No real cities to speak of and nothing but land as far as the eye could see. But Gods be damned, Wyatt, that was the most beautiful land I'd ever seen. The grass was greener than any shade of green I'd seen before. The hills, they rolled on and on for miles looking for all the world like a green quilt. The earth was dark and rich in a lot of areas so there were farms scattered among the clans. That's how they divided the land in those days, family clans. It was pretty complicated to understand at first but, for the most part, these folks were farmers and family men." Decker drained his glass once more and, after two unsuccessful attempts to remove the lid, Wyatt opened the bottle and poured him another glass.

"You okay?"

"I'm just fine. I settled in the more southern region among the Brigantes. That was the clan name. At first they didn't know what to think of me, I suppose. I mean, there were folks coming and going through the ports, that was right outside of what's now called Dublin. That was a fun time. I learned, after spending a few years near the port, how to talk like them, dress like them, and to blend in as best I could. There were times when a scuffle between Gauls and locals would break out. That's when it got fun. But other than that, there weren't much happening. I heard rumors about the different clans further north and I decided to pack it up and continue on my adventure."

"You went north then? Weren't you scared?" Wyatt asked.

"Nar, not scared. It was a peaceful place. I'd go days without seeing anyone. There were a lot of cows though. Cows everywhere, that was the way you could tell a wealthy man from a poor one." Decker took a sip from his glass. "So I decided to get me some cows," Wyatt broke into fits of laughter.

"You? You bought a bunch of cows? My father owns a cattle ranch. That's a pretty tough business," Wyatt said and took a sip of his whiskey. Decker eyed him carefully and leaned forward.

"I don't hear much from you about your family. Why's that? Where's your cattle ranching Da?" Wyatt turned the glass around in his hand and studied the brown liquid carefully.

"That's because my father doesn't speak to me anymore," he answered quietly. "He told me a long time ago, right when I turned eighteen, to get out and stay gone."

"What for?"

"Because, Decker, there are a lot of people these days who hate what I am. It doesn't jive with their moral superiority." Wyatt looked at Decker with obvious pain in his eyes. Decker's loud belch broke the silence.

"'Scuse me." He slapped Wyatt on the back and smiled. "Fuck him."

Wyatt smiled and nodded his head as he raised his glass to drink.

"Here, I'll do a toast," Decker said as he struggled to his feet. Wyatt, still smiling, stood as well. Decker cleared his throat and raised his glass into the air with a dramatic flourish that slopped some of the brown liquid onto his arm. He licked his lips and cleared his throat again before he spoke.

"To Wyatt, my mate, my buddy, my pal,
Cursed with a father who was fucking foul,
You grew into a handsome man, brave and true,
Wyatt, I'm honored to have a friend like you."

Both men took a drink from their glasses, although
Decker drained his while Wyatt took a small sip. Decker
plopped back into his chair with little grace but Wyatt stood
over him. His eyes held unshed tears he tried to blink away.

"Thank you," he said. Decker, lighting another
cigarette, nodded his head and motioned for him to sit.

"Something I've learned in my long life, Wyatt –
Everyone has something that hurts them. Everyone. There
ain't no shame in it. But there's a sadness hidden away in
everyone's shadow. Some like to pretend it's not there but
it is. If you try to run from your own shadow, you won't
get very far. Just know it's there and that it'll always be
there. It's a part of who you are."

Wyatt silently nodded and turned his attention back
to the notebook.

"So, how long did you stay in Ireland? That
must've been quite a change for you after Rome and
Egypt," he said.

"Aye, it was a big change but, after years of getting
to know the folks, I came to see how they were just like the
rest of the world. There were some good ones and some
bad ones. But I liked these folks better. They were simple,
compared to the Romans. Wealth and power weren't
necessarily their ambition. They worked together, for the
most part, as a community. It reminded me of the army,
although, without much fighting. Oh sure, there were little
scuffles between clans over some business with a cow or
land disputes but, all in all, those were nice quiet years." He
took another drink from his glass and flicked his cigarette
into the yard. Decker motioned for Wyatt to fill his glass
again and he rubbed his face with his hands.

Wyatt silently poured more whiskey and handed the glass to him. Decker was aware his hands were shaky and he felt agitated. Too agitated to stay still, he stood up, glass in hand, and began to pace.

"I'd been in Ireland for many, many years by the time your Jesus was born and died. Small snippets came to us, many well after the fact, but no one really paid much mind to it. I could feel it though, the Otherness of the times. There were many, many non-humans roaming around in those days. It's hard to explain to someone who's...normal. But I could feel things happening." He said as he paced around and almost tripped on the leg of Wyatt's chair.

"You weren't curious about it all?" Wyatt asked.

"Nope." He shook his head. "I could tell where they were from and I have no love for that sort. They scared me a little. I'd seen them and felt them about before but I avoided them. I guess they avoided me too. But I also knew when they were around because bad things always happened. It was always something. Some kind of devastation, mass murder, war, you name it. Nope," he took another drink, "I was pleased to stay right where I was. Nobody bothered us there and I was happy with that."

"I can't picture you living the quiet life, Decker," Wyatt said with a smile. Decker smiled and shrugged his shoulders.

"You'd be surprised. I did live quite the quiet life for a time. I had friends to drink with and a bed to sleep in. However, I've got to say," he turned to Wyatt and bowed slightly. "The beer has improved since those days. So for that, humanity has my eternal thanks." Wyatt laughed. Decker frowned, downed his glass, and returned to his seat. He waved off another refill; the whiskey was already having a serious effect on him. His face was numb and everything beyond arm's length was getting blurry. He still had much to tell. Wyatt sat silent. Decker could feel the man's gaze almost as heavy as the rock in his stomach.

"There was a time, after I'd been settled in my home for a while, that the folks I knew died out and others moved into their homes. They knew me, and I think they knew I wasn't all together normal, but they usually let me be. I helped everyone I could and, in those days, that's all that really mattered. Were their little urchins fed? Were their wives fat and satisfied? Were they getting enough beer? All the main concerns of the day. I didn't associate with the higher born families anymore. I liked the regular folk. They were good, fun, people. What I wanted to tell you tonight, mate, is the story of how I met Cliona."

"Who's Cliona?" Wyatt asked.

Decker didn't answer right away. He stared into the dark sky, into the distant past.

"I had my hands full with my humble cattle ranch. Damn cows needed tending constantly, I found out. I hired me a few young lads to come help and, in return, I fed them and they slept in a small hut next to the barn. Lorcan and Quinn. Both good, strong lads who came from families who couldn't really afford to feed them anymore. Plus, they wanted to get out on their own. A common thing, I suppose. Lorcan was a huge, beefy fellow covered in hair and he didn't talk much. But, he saw a lot and I liked that. Quinn was smaller, no less strong but talked all the damn time. If he wasn't talking, he was making up songs. He was good in the kitchen too, so he'd cook our meals on the outside fire and we lived pretty happily there, the three of us.

"One day, the boys were splitting firewood, Quinn was singing, keeping time with Lorcan's swings, when I heard a noise that was unusual. A scream. I was stacking the wood when I stopped to listen but couldn't hear anything over Quinn's yodeling. 'Shut your mouth, Quinn. You hear that?' I asked him. Both boys shook their heads no and all three of us stood still to listen. Then, I heard it again and I ran towards the scream. The boys hadn't heard it, but they came running after me anyhow. That was noble of them."

"Your hearing is better than ours?" Wyatt asked.

"Aye. It is. I ran through the field and down into the nearby forest. There was a stream that ran through there and I figured someone might've fallen in and got themselves hurt or something. As I got closer, though, I saw there were four men and a girl. Two had the girl's arms, one was right in her face, and the other was holding her head back with a fistful of her hair. 'Oy!' I yelled to 'em. 'What you doing to the lass? Let her go.' I said. They stopped talking to the girl and looked at me. The one who was in the girl's face stepped in front and told me it weren't none of my business and to go on home."

"Which you did right away, right?" Wyatt asked, teasing. Decker snorted.

"I saw the girl was crying, her basket of roots she'd gathered spilled all over the ground, and her dress was all torn. I didn't like the way the men were touching her either. 'Let her go. Or I'll make you.' I told 'em. They laughed and thought it was all good fun, I guess. The one in front came at me and I clocked him pretty good. Knocked him out cold with one hit to the temple. His friends weren't laughing after that. They dropped the girl in the mud and all three came after me. It was a good fight, one of 'em was a big man."

"He wasn't a match for you though, was he?"

"Nope. I had them all well in hand by the time Lorcan and Quinn made it there. They jumped in at the end and helped make sure the girl was alright and the blokes on the ground didn't get back up."

"You killed them all?" Wyatt asked.

"Nar. I didn't kill them. Just made sure they weren't waking up anytime soon. I had one in a nice tight choker hold and Lorcan gave the other one a swift kick to the face. That did it," Decker laughed. "The girl was trying to pick up all her food she dropped but she was crying too much. I told Quinn to help her, since he's the gentlest of the three of us. He helped her gather it all and she seemed alright after that. No real harm. She had long blonde hair and real fair skin. A real looker without the tears and mud stains everywhere. I thought, maybe, she'd be a good match for Quinn. All the girls liked him so, I figured, she wouldn't be any different. Boy, was I wrong there." Decker let out a half-hearted laugh.

"It was you she wanted, right?" Decker's mouth twisted in an odd mix between grimace and laugh.

"Aye. It was the strangest thing. A real pretty girl like that, she could've had any lad she wanted. But a couple days after we helped her, here she came walking up to my door with a basket of food. Gifts she said, for me. I didn't know what to do, really. My only involvement with women, in the past, had always been whores. She weren't no whore. Young girl, all freshly grown and pretty as can be. Quinn thought it was right funny that she came to thank me and give me stuff. She thanked me for my help and told me her name, Cliona. When she left, she gave me a nice, shy smile before she turned to leave. The next day she did it again. She brought me bread, I think. She asked if she could see the cows and I told her, 'Sure. They're right over there.' and I went inside. I didn't want her around. The boys laughed and smiled too much when they saw her coming up the hill."

"You didn't take her to see your cows?" Wyatt asked, laughing. "How unchivalrous of you."

"You're right. I weren't no gentleman, that's for sure. She visited with some cows, bid the boys a good day, then went on her way. The next day she came back again. I told her, 'I thank you for the cake, but I got work to do.' But she just followed me to where I was chopping wood.

Pretty soon, she was stacking the wood for me as I cut it. Oh, Lorcan and Quinn thought that was a riot. They stood back, snickering and elbowing each other while they whispered their jokes. 'Now see here, Lass, You've thanked me enough and there's no need for you to come back here.' I told her that. She just smiled and, get this Wyatt, she told me, 'We'll discuss it on the morrow.' Then she left." Decker laughed.

"Oh, she was hardheaded." Wyatt said.

"Aye. Sure enough she was back the next day and the day after that. No matter what I said, no matter what I told her, she just kept coming back. She'd bring food, flowers, and even made me a cloth for my table. I didn't know what to do with her!"

"Sure you did," Wyatt said with a smirk.

"I wasn't thinking about her that way. But she cooked good and even prepared dinner for me and boys a few times. I don't know, I got used to her coming around after a while. Then, one afternoon, she asked me to take a walk with her. I knew by then there weren't no way I'd get out of it if she wanted to do it, so I did. We walked along the hills and she chatted about her Da, who was a farmer and her Ma who taught her how to do all those damn girly things. I didn't say much, but she said enough for the both of us. On our walk, we ended up in the same place where I'd first met her, by the stream. She got real quiet then. I asked if she was all right but she shook her head. Then she told me, one of those men was one her Ma wanted her to marry. Imagine that, Wyatt? Imagine having to marry a man like that."

"I can't...that's horrible."

"She cried a little and told me she didn't want to marry the man, obviously. 'Donagh, I don't know what to do,' she says and then she's crying into my shirt. I didn't know what to do, so I just held the poor girl as she cried."

"Aww, see, you really are a soft old bear." Wyatt said. Decker shrugged his shoulders and lit another cigarette. He motioned for Wyatt to fill his glass and continued on, whiskey in hand.

"When she stopped crying, she looked up at me with these big, soft, blue eyes. It was the first time I'd looked at a woman and thought, This is the most beautiful creature I'd ever seen. And she truly was. I told her she had pretty eyes, I didn't know what else to say. She smiled and said she liked mine as well. That was new. Usually everybody gets scared of me when they see my eyes close up. But not Cliona." He took another hearty drink and licked his lips. "I remember, when we walked back to the house, she held my arm. I liked that."

Chapter Six

"She carried on coming to visit for a good long while. Every afternoon we'd take a walk and talk about anything and everything. She was smart and real quick of wit. Quick to laugh and easy on the eyes, I admit it, I enjoyed spending time with her. But her Ma, her Ma was trying to hurry the wedding up. Cliona was terrified. I wanted to help but she said there weren't much I could do. I didn't like that," Decker said.

"You could have married her," Wyatt said gently. Decker met Wyatt's eyes and smiled sadly. Flicking the ashes from his cigarette, he continued.

"One day, the rains started and didn't let up. It was terrible. Whole fields were under water and my cows had all run for higher ground. Cliona was there helping to get the other animals all safe and dry in the barn. The boys were staying in the barn to play their games and drink, I suppose. It weren't possible for Cliona to walk home in the rains so I had to invite her in to stay. She seemed pleased about it all. We ate dinner, talked a lot--well she talked a lot, I listened. I found out she had a talent for storytelling as well. She told me one that night, one just for me. About a fair haired lass that was saved from evil. I do believe she made that one up, but she never told me."

"She sounds lovely."

"After dinner and some ale, I realized I'd have to sleep in the barn with the boys. I didn't fancy that because I liked my little bed with all my comforts. I very well couldn't send Cliona to sleep in the barn, so, I told her I'd sleep in front of the fire and gave her my bed."

"Oh, it's gonna get saucy now, I can tell," Wyatt said with a smile.

"Hush. Everything was fine, just fine, until she got out of bed, wrapped in my blanket, and joined me on the floor. She didn't say nothing at first. She just leaned in, real slow, and kissed me. I've kissed a lot of women in my days. A lot. But that kiss was different. I wanted to give in… she was so sweet and pure, you know? I thought, Decker, what are you doing? She's a pretty, young maid and here you are…a… monster," Decker closed his eyes and exhaled. "I told her, 'Cliona, I'm not what you think I am. I'm different. Dangerous.' She smiled real sweet and kissed me again. She wouldn't listen when I tried to tell her I wasn't…wasn't…"

"That you weren't what?"

"Good. But she wouldn't let me finish. We, uh, you know…that night."

"I knew it! Saucy," Wyatt laughed.

"All right now, I'm trying to be serious. It was a beautiful night. She'd never had a man before so it was something different, for me anyhow."

"You can spare me the details, hetro sex kinda grosses me out," Wyatt said with a good natured smile.

"All right, I'll spare you the details but it was a pleasant experience. We spent the night by the fire and I woke up with a beautiful woman, who was not a whore, in my arms. Of course, the next day I felt heavy. I didn't want her to go home. I wanted her to stay, there in my little house with me. But her family was certainly looking for her and worried by that time, so she hurried off, but not before she kissed me goodbye."

"Oh my God, this is just too precious. So what happened? Did she marry that horrible man after all? Did you see her again? Come on, you're telling this story too slowly," Wyatt said.

"I'm telling it slow because it's important. The most important story I've got to tell you. So shut your trap. Where was I?" He took another drink and scratched his chin. "Right, so the next day she didn't come back and the boys decided to go looking for her."

"The boys? Or you?"

"The boys were fond of her, but they knew she fancied me. It was Quinn who said we ought to go check on her. So, the three of us took off down the hill and I sent Quinn ahead to ask where her family lived. It weren't long before he came running back in a dither. In between breaths, he told me the tale. Apparently, Cliona's Ma had Cliona locked in the house and wouldn't let her out. Said she was keeping her there until she agreed to marry the bastard who hurt her."

"Oh no."

"Oh yes. I mean, it wasn't unheard of for the times. Marriages were for alliances, money, safety, all sorts of reasons. But the thought of her being forced to marry that man that tried to hurt her…just burned me up. We made our way to the community down the hill and Quinn showed me the little house that was Cliona's family home. It was a one room mud and grass hut with a thatched roof. The windows were just holes cut out of the walls. I hated seeing it because she was too fine to be in such a place. After seeing the wealth and splendor of Rome, I wanted more for her. Her Da was standing outside arguing with a fat woman I found out was her Ma. When we walked up, they stopped arguing and looked at us.

"Her Da was real pissed and her Ma was in tears. They asked what I wanted and who I was. I told 'em, 'I'm here to see Cliona.' Her Ma started yelling, telling us to go away and her Da stepped back and was taking measure of me. The boys hung back and let me do the talking. Instead of talking to them, I started calling for Cliona. I wanted her to know I'd come for her. After a few calls, I heard her inside calling my name." Decker wiped his hand down his face and stared at his bare feet. "I can still hear her calling my name. Not my real name, mind you, but the name that was mine back then.

"I asked her Da, 'Can I see her?' and he said yes straight away and her Ma said no. But I went to the door with her Da beside me and he opened the door to let me in. It weren't nothing bad about the place but it was colorless and felt sad. I looked around and saw Cliona sitting on the floor in the back with her head in her hands, crying. I walked across the small house and, right when I stood over her, she looked up. Those beautiful blue eyes were swollen and red. She was dirty and so sad that it made me angry. I reached out for her and picked her right up off the floor. That's when I realized her Ma had tied her to the bench with rope like a damn cow.

"Well, I ripped that rope from the bench quick as you please and turned, with her in my arms, to face her Da. I told him, 'She can't marry that man. He's a right evil prick. I caught him and his mates trying to hurt her not long ago. Had to help her then like I am now.' Her Da, he was a good man. He just stared at me. He had this real full, bushy beard and mustache. Hardly any face left on the man that wasn't covered in hair," Decker laughed. "But we looked at each other and after a little bit, he nodded. 'You care for my Cliona?' he asked me. 'What sort of man are ya?' he asked."

"Well that's a loaded question." Wyatt said.

"Aye. I told him I had a house and plenty of cattle, more cattle than they had by far. Before I knew it, Wyatt, I was telling her Da I wanted to take care of her. While she clung to me and cried, I knew I couldn't disappoint her. I told her Da I'd marry her."

"You what?" Wyatt exclaimed. He had long since neglected to write anything down, he was so transfixed by the tale. Decker blinked furiously, fighting the tears that threatened to spill down his face.

"She held me tighter and her Da stepped out of the way. We three walked to where the boys and Cliona's Ma stood. That was an uncomfortable moment. Her Da informed everyone Cliona and I were to marry and all hell broke loose. The boys guffawed and slapped me on the back and her Ma wailed like a damn banshee. Apparently, I found out some time later, Cliona's family was having a tough go of things and her Ma made a bargain with the man, Ardan, for some cattle in exchange for Cliona's hand. As was the usual custom."

"You got married, Decker? I can't…I didn't think you were the marrying type," Wyatt said in disbelief.

"I married Cliona the next day. She insisted we make it official and be done with it. She was practical, my wife. The ceremony was a simple affair compared to the pomp and ritual of other weddings I've seen. They did that hand fasting thing, you know, tied our hands with rope and said a bunch of nonsense. I don't remember everything. I just remember looking at her, with a circle of flowers on her head." He used his finger to draw a circle over his head. "She was real pretty in her blue dress. Same blue as her eyes…" His voice trailed off as the tears that had threatened to fall slowly snaked their way down his cheeks. He wiped at them absently and let out a slow breath. He couldn't look at Wyatt, not out of shame or embarrassment, but out of fear.

"We were married for five years. For those five years I was a happy, normal man. We took care of the cattle, the boys and I, and Cliona took care of our house. We were content." His voice caught in his throat and held his head in his hands. His breath was labored as he attempted to gain control once more. "I don't know why she didn't tell me…"

"Tell you what?" Wyatt asked softly.

"She didn't tell me for some time, thought she'd surprise me with it. She was with child and I hadn't a clue. She told me, over dinner, 'Donagh, you're going to be a Da.' And I knew it…I just knew it then it wouldn't end well. I begged her to drink the herbal drinks women drink to, you know, not have babies. But she went off on in a right state when I said that. Her Da and I, we were good pals, he told me not to worry. See, he thought I was worried our child would have my, as he called it, affliction of the eyes. Affliction of the eyes..." Decker chuckled and wiped away fresh tears.

"What happened, Decker?" Wyatt asked softly, pain and fear in his voice.

"She was real big with child. I was terrified she was too big but she kept laughing at me, telling me I didn't know anything about babies and to shut me mouth." He let out a barking laugh "She was right about that. Damn mystery to me how a woman can have another living thing inside her and be happy about it. But she was over the moon about it. She rubbed her belly and talked to the baby inside her like it could hear her. She even made me touch her belly when it moved. But she didn't know what I knew. She didn't know what I really was and she didn't know about my brothers. I'd stay up into the night, begging the Gods, any God, to spare her. I begged them to give her a normal baby. One without my affliction of the eyes." His tears fell freely but he made no move to wipe them away or hide them.

"The baby...was it...what happened?" Wyatt reached out and laid a hand on Decker's shoulder. Decker's head dropped and he took a deep breath. When he exhaled, he looked up into the night sky and studied the twinkling stars above.

"One morning, I woke earlier than she did. She was fast asleep in our little bed. I didn't want to wake her, so I went to take a piss and fetch her fresh water. When I returned, she hadn't moved and I just thought she was real tired from the baby and all, you know? Hours went by...I went to check on her and saw that she slept still. But, just as I was turning to leave, I saw something that stopped me cold. A red stain was on the blankets and I could smell blood. I rushed to shake her, to try to wake her up, but she was so pale...so cold." Decker absently wiped the tears from his face. "I screamed for Quinn and Lorcan to fetch some women from the village. I tried to wake her." His voice caught in his throat and he threw his glass of whiskey down onto the ground. The brown liquid spread like golden tears across the wood.

"She…was she…did Cliona…?" Wyatt's voice broke and he let out a rumbling sob. The look on Decker's face told him the end of the tale.

"Aye, my Cliona died in her sleep. The women that came, including her Ma, tried all they could but there weren't nothing to do to help her. They said it was the baby…grew too big for her and she couldn't carry it. It killed her. I killed her." Decker's head dropped and he wept silently into his hands. Wyatt stood and went to his friend's side. He sank to his knees, tears running down his face, and placed an arm around his shoulders.

Footsteps made them both look up to see Theo and Vasha approaching. Without a word, they walked toward Decker and embraced him. The four men, each with pain in their hearts knowing all too well the agony of loss, held onto each other in silence.

Chapter Seven

Decker slept late the next morning. He had no idea when he stumbled, with Vasha's help, to the renovated shed to sleep among the plump pillows his brother loved so much. His head pounded with the beat of his heart and he marveled at the power of too much drink. Vasha was nowhere to be seen as he stood slowly and stretched his aching back. The pillows, for all their beauty and color, weren't as comfortable as a bed. He'd rather sleep under the stars on the hard ground than sleep on those lumpy things again.

For the rest of the day, Decker walked slower and avoided direct sunlight. Hangovers were a bitch and he'd really tied one on hard the previous night. However, an odd sense of peace lay on him as he helped himself to food in Mela's kitchen and lots and lots of water. The burden he'd carried for so long of his dead wife was shared with others now. Her memory was no longer as painful as it once was. His pain, once bottled and ignored, was purged and all that was left was a wound that only the love of his friends and brothers could heal. But he knew now it would heal.

When Mela got home from work that afternoon, Decker saw to her sword training. She very nearly got the better of him a few times. He claimed it was due to his previous night of drinking but the truth was she was getting better. He was indeed slower but she was faster than usual.

Wyatt came, as Decker assumed he would, and set up his notebook and recorder in silence. Although he appreciated Wyatt's presence, he really hated the heavy silence.

"Oy, you're uncharacteristically quiet this evening. Cat got your tongue?" Decker smiled. Wyatt met his eyes briefly before returning to flipping pages in his notebook.

"I just don't know what to say after... well, after what you told me. How did you go on? What did you do after..." Wyatt's words trailed off and he shook his head. "I don't know how you survived that. I would've died."

"Oh, I wanted to die. Trust me, I longed for death after I put her in the ground. I remember we buried her in the exact same place where we first met. Beneath a tree marked with flowers and stones, I said my last goodbye to her. I left my home and never went back. I took what little mattered to me, of course, but I left the rest. I couldn't stay there where we lived together and where she died."

"I can understand that. Where did you go?"

"Roaming around. Drinking until I passed out and ended up back in the ports. I took a ship to the Island of the Brits. I don't remember much about that time. Barely even remember the ship I took, come to think of it. Most likely, I was drunk as a skunk. But the real change came for me when I met up with a group that I had a lot in common with."

"Who were they?'

"Vikings. They didn't mind my sullen ways or the fact that I drank a bit too much far too often. No, they saw how well I handled a sword and I was quickly taken in. Never as one of them, mind you, but I fought alongside them. I knew their language, as there were Vikings in Ireland here and there. Not many where I lived but there was a common tongue. I fought anyone and everyone I could during that time. I longed for death and I thought it was a grand idea to go out in a battle. Didn't much care who did the deed really, as long as I died in the end. But, obviously, no one was good enough to strike the killing blow. Sure, I ended up with my fair share of injuries and pain, but never death. Even thought about doing it myself once or twice..."

"That's not you, Decker,"

"No, you're right. Going out in battle is the way I'm supposed to leave this world. Not by my own hand."

"Can you die? I mean, you obviously don't age like…like…"

"Like normal people?" Decker smiled.

"Well, that's a crude way of putting it. But yeah, you don't age like I do."

"Oh, you're normal now, are you? Right, I'm quite certain plenty of blokes have a best girl, who they don't fuck. Good pals who aren't all together human and a bloody Angel twittering about. Sure. You're as normal as rain." They both laughed.

"All right, you have me there. Like other, more average, humans."

"Theo and I had this discussion not too long ago. About death. We're not sure if we can die in any way other than something violent and bloody. My guess is, if I lose my head, I'll be dead. But since that's still on nice and tight," he shrugged, "I'll keep on going."

"More talk of lobbing off heads." Wyatt smiled and rolled his eyes.

"I've relieved quite a few folks of the burden of a head over the years . It's tricky business getting it off in one stroke. You need to make sure your sword is nice and sharp."

Wyatt held his hand up for Decker to stop. "That's enough of that. Tell that stuff to Mela, I'm sure it'll come in handy one day. Not me. I couldn't do it. No way."

"Don't underestimate yourself, Wyatt. Plenty of us say that but you never know what you're capable of until you're faced with an extreme circumstance."

Wyatt shrugged his shoulders and didn't respond. Decker noted the stubborn set of his mouth and snorted. Fine, the lad won't fight by choice. That was both a liability and an asset.

"So, Vikings, huh? That sounds…brutal." Wyatt said, raising an eyebrow.

"They were conquerors, that's for certain. There's a lot of similarities between them and the Romans. Not in the ways of the people but in the desire to conquer and control. Rome wanted folks to assimilate and become Romans. Vikings made their living pillaging the coasts. They wanted the wealth of other countries and they needed the resources. I respected them a bit more, I guess. A brutal people and they didn't pretend to be anything other than what they were. But I tell you what," he said with a smile, "I got over my fear of ships right quick."

"I was about to ask that. Did you learn how to swim finally?"

"Aye. Swim, fish, hunt properly and to fight like a Viking. Oh, you know sword play is generally the same thing any way you look at it, kill your opponent. But each group went about it a different way. I liked the swords well enough but it was carrying the shield that hindered me a bit. But….you do what you must, I suppose. While the others raped and pillaged, I looked for someone, anyone, who could challenge me. No one could beat me in combat and after a good long time, I stopped looking. I don't know what did it really, nothing in particular. I just stopped looking for my death and decided to wait for it to come. To will it to me. But it never did.

"I spent years upon years fighting with Viking clans. Different ones over the years, and after an appropriate amount of time, I'd disappear and they'd assume I died. I'd spent a good while living on the smaller islands, sometimes all alone, before I'd find somewhere to hang my hat again."

"Your hat…Now that you mention it, it looks pretty old. Where'd you get it?"

"That's a story for later. I'll get there." He reached for a cigar in the box beside him and lit the end. He puffed on it until the smoke encircled them both and Wyatt waved his hand in front of his face. "I don't rightly remember how long I lived that way. Coming in and out of the life way up there, everything just runs together. I know it was bloody cold during winter. Snow was deep and I was more than happy to catch a ship to more southern destinations to pass the winters. But, like all things, that too ended."

"Where'd you end up when it ended?"

"What's now referred to as Scotland. I liked that place, it reminded me a lot of the people of Ireland. Good people but the influence of the Romans kept a lingering stench of greed and backstabbing amongst the noblemen. Lots of battles happened, but I stayed pretty well away from that for some time. There was a small island, off the coast, where I spent most of my time. I made a nice comfy hut and used my newly discovered fishing skills to survive. I knew a thing or two about managing animals as well, but it was sheep this time. Just a few, but I managed fine on my own. I think I spent too much time alone then, come to think on it."

"Well, I can understand that. After everything that happened."

Decker picked his nose as he thought about what came after his time as a Viking. In truth, it all ran together. The cold, the wind, the sunshine that he loved and the smell of the sea. As he flicked a rather large green blob into the yard, he tried to remember when he left the island. Many times he would go to the big island, as the locals called it, for supplies and materials, but he stayed that way for an incredibly long time. He closed one nostril with his finger and blew out the other side causing a large glob of green mucus to land at his feet.

"You could blow your nose into a tissue. Just a suggestion," Wyatt said, notably not looking at him as he repeated the process on the other side.

"What for? This way works just the same," he gave his nose one last, hard, blow before he wiped his hand on his new blue jeans. "I don't remember years or nothing but I did end up with a right fun lot eventually. I met a man by the name of Grog. Not his real name, but that's what they called him.

"Scottish?"

"Nar, he was....what you call that place now? Right on the Baltic Sea..." Decker scratched his head and scrunched up his face in concentration. "Oh, fuck me, can't remember now. But Grog belonged to the Curonian people. Those blokes there, the first real pirates. I'm talking battles at sea and an insatiable lust for violence."

"Let me guess, you joined them on a few sea adventures?"

"Aye. I did. Grog and I met drinking in a tavern one evening. I rather liked old Grog," he laughed. "Grog told me, after just tossing his cookies all over some whore's lap, that I ought to come along with him and be free. 'Got to be a free man, Dark,' he kept saying. That's what he called me, Dark. He couldn't say my name all that well, so he just gave me a new one," Decker shrugged. "It was fine with me as I hadn't really gone by a specific name for years. So, Dark it was."

"Dark?" Wyatt laughed and wrote the name down.

"The next morning when we woke up, still in the tavern, I gathered up all my wordly goods, which weren't all that much, and headed out with Grog to his ship. Once onboard I found his mates were a friendly lot, more than my previous mates, I guess. Or, I was more welcoming, not sure, now that I think about it. But Grog was a good pal. He helped me learn a bit of the language--it was the Germanic language but I picked it up alright. All I really needed to know were certain words, the rest weren't necessary. I learned how to say 'more drink' right off." Both men laughed.

"They just accepted you in their groups, huh? It seems odd that such a violent people would be so welcoming to a stranger."

"Well, I ain't a regular guy, now am I? I imagine it's my eyes. Either folks were frightened of them or they were intrigued. The ones who weren't afraid of me, saw me as an asset. Those who were afraid of me were afraid for good reason. I stayed clear of the folks who were scared. No good comes from being the thing folks are afraid of. Fear is a man's most basic instinct. Survival, you know? If they fear you, really fear you, they'll try to kill you, it's a natural thing. No matter how good a warrior I am, I can't take on a mob of frightened villagers with swords, pitchforks, and torches intent on killing the object of their fear."

"Yikes...never thought about it that way before. I don't know, I guess I see you as indestructible."

"Well, I'm not. And I ain't stupid neither. Where was I?" he took a puff from his cigar and tilted his head to the side. "Right, Grog. I settled in his village and soon, I was going out on raids left and right. I didn't even bother making my own house. I stayed on the ship almost all the time. There were many, many ships but I liked one in particular. I had space to sleep and plenty to eat. But what I enjoyed the most, what made me feel alive again, were the battles between ships. Oh, Wyatt, I wish I could tell it as well as I remember it." He stood up to make room for his exaggerated flailing of his arms. "This one time, me, Grog and the crew were headed out to capture a fishing boat, you see." He bit the edge of his cigar to hold it in his mouth as he spoke. "We saw the boat on the horizon and quickly steered our course toward her, 'Let's go, you whore's sons!' the Captain called to us. We gathered our swords to make ready to board but before we reached her port side, right behind us, came another ship. Ho Ho! We had ourselves quite the battle! The archers fired flaming arrows back and forth," he mimicked, ducking side to side. "They were falling all around us. Those cabin boys had one job to do, put all the fires out. They ran around with jugs of water and just put out little fires here and there."

"Isn't that dangerous? I mean, those kids were in real danger, weren't they?" Wyatt asked.

"Sure," he shrugged. "More than a few caught an arrow in the gut. Once we got close enough to actually fight the other ship, we saw it was a German ship. That was good fight, that was. Those fellows went through, what Grog and his folks called, the Slaughter of Souls."

"What's that mean?"

"They were overrun by the very powerful Catholic church. Grog's people considered it a great insult to the soul to convert, I guess. Or they called it that because the church was starting so many wars in her name, I don't know. But that's what they called it. These Germans, they were doing the Church's work, converting the heathens – us. Well, I weren't having none of that and neither were they. That ship got away before we could board her but not too long after, there was a real fight. We went out, much the same way, but saw loads of ships on the horizon. The Captain, I don't remember him, he turned the boat around, went back to shore and gathered up a whole fleet of Curonion ships. We headed back out and managed to engage them in a nasty face-off. They were looking for us, you see. Getting revenge for the other ship that was attacked."

"What was that like? A battle at sea?"

"Thrilling, in a word. The salty air smacked you right in the face and made you focus. Our ships were fast and our archers better aims. By design, we circled the German fleet and closed in until we had them nestled right where we wanted 'em. Oh, they put up a fight, no doubt. Me and Grog went on the first wave to the nearest ship. We had ropes and swung from our ship straight to theirs. From there," he mimicked a sword battle. "We fought them nice and close up. Funny thing was, Grog didn't bother always killing them. A lot of the time, he'd knock 'em off the boat and laugh as they went down into the water. Most of them drowned because of their armor. It was just too heavy to swim in. We wore a different sort of armor when we were out on the ships. We took one ship after another and before long, we met the other half of our party that had fought their way from the other side. In all, we captured thirty ships that day."

"How many ships were you?"

"Eight." Decker smiled proudly and slapped his leg when he laughed. "It was a sight to see for sure." He sat back down and stretched out his legs in front of him. Decker remembered the smells of the sea and the glory of the battle won. He could hear the men still, however faintly, cheering for their captain and their homeland. He never understood all of the words, but he felt their pride as they escorted thirty foreign ships back to their home harbor. The vision of the children running alongside the docks hailing their return was always a treat as well. Decker never cared for children much, but the young lads were treated as small men and he approved of that.

"How long were you there?" Wyatt asked, interrupting his thoughts.

"I left when I saw it was inevitable that the Curonians were succumbing to The Slaughter of their Souls."

"The...Oh, right. The Christian Church finally won them over, huh?" Decker cocked his head from side to side and made a face.

"It was a tricky thing, really. They...we...pissed off quite a number of folks, it was only a matter of time before it all came back around to bite our asses."

"What do you mean?"

"Well, we pissed off the Germans, the Dornish and a few others because of our nautical adventures. They were coming together to make some sort of convert or die campaign. Stupid shits. Pretty soon, Grog's people were discussing bringing in some monks. Those shits." He stood up again. "They were real bastards. Never have I seen a greater example of deceit in a congregation of men. They took all the money, controlled the food supplies and pretty much took over the rule of the people."

"The Slaughter of Souls…"

"Aye. Slaughtered like a lamb before a feast." Decker sat back down and tried to relight his cigar. He remembered the young boys, once so full of life and vigor, grown to starving young men. He watched them lose their fire and zest for life as they kneeled and scraped inside stone churches before men in robes. The memories made him feel ill. Worse than that, he felt the familiar squeeze of guilt for leaving them. Because he did leave them, abruptly, early one morning in the summer. The previous night, Decker didn't drink and watched the sadness that'd spread throughout the village. He wanted to flee the dark cloud of misery, so he did. Before the sun came up, Decker packed his belongings and headed out to catch a fishing ship. No one questioned him as he left; they'd become accustomed to his comings and goings. But this was a going. He knew his time with Grog's people was at an end as he watched the coast slip away from the rail of the ship.

It took him years to find another place in the world. More years than he could count. Living on a ship or in ports made the passing days and months blend in with the rest. He smelled of stale ale and sweat. He slept on ships or on rooftops to pass the time. The further south he traveled, the more opportunities came his way to work on a ship. But sailors were superstitious to the bone. Too many times he was denied access to a crew because they were afraid at the sight of him. They'd be interested in his size and apparent strength right away. The captains or the first mate would be dazzled by his knowledge of ships. However, when it came down to it, they looked him in the eyes and said no. Sometimes it was with an apology. Other times at sword point. Either way, he had no ship to call home and no crew. It was the longest time he'd ever been without the security of friends or comrades-in-arms. The religious fervor had spread and the fear of the people rose along with their religious conversion. Decker soon learned to avoid the ports that traded with ships involved in the Crusades.

"It was good that I spent most of my time either on a ship or alone at that point. The Plague was killing folks all over by that time. Scores of folks died, bodies piled up in villages, and everyone was very afraid."

"I bet. Can you get sick?" Wyatt asked.

"Not sure, really. I never did, so I guess not. But I watched the folks drop like flies. The sickness made its way to the ports and spread on the ships. But the stink was a little better closer to the sea. Nothing worse than smelling rotten corpses and burning flesh. The smart ones burned the bodies. The dumb bastards left them in piles for days and all the while, folks kept dying, and the reek got worse. Except on a ship. If someone died on a ship, they wrapped him up quick as can be and plopped his ass into the sea."

"That seems like the way to go in that situation."

"It sure was. It was actually because of the Plague I finally found a place to hang my hat, so to speak. Although, not this hat." He held up the tattered black bowler hat and made it spin on his finger. "I found my way as south as I could go on my own. It was a little fishing village that had lost a lot of their men who knew how to work a ship. It was on the Italian coast, so the weather was nice and the sun kept me warm during the day. I stayed there for a long time. One day, this man was on the docks yelling for any able bodied men to help him fish. Somebody had died, his son, his brother, fuck if I know, but I answered his call. I don't think he really wanted to hire me, but he was kind of out of options. He looked me up and down, then pointed to his ship and off we went. I fished with him for a short while. He didn't talk much, I remember that. But we caught fish and sent the kids that survived the sickness to sell the fish to the villages nearby. It was a quiet time, the longest I ever went without fighting," Decker laughed. "But in those days, one didn't go long without some sort of a fight. It just so happened I had a run-in with a group of blokes that would come to be my new brothers."

"I can only imagine where this is going. Let me guess," Wyatt laughed and punched Decker's shoulder. "You became a full blown pirate."

"You're one smart man," Decker smiled. "I did in fact become a part of an industrious, dedicated and highly violent group of men. They came into port one night. I was sleeping on the ship and saw them quietly sail in. I watched the men for a while as they went here and there. I could tell they were disciplined and tight with one another. I wanted that." He looked down at the hat in his hands and brushed invisible dust from the top. "I approached one of the men and he told me to fuck off." Decker laughed and Wyatt groaned.

"Oh no! You didn't kill him, did you?"

"Now, why would you ask such a thing? I don't kill everyone who tells me to fuck off, Wyatt. If I did, there'd be a lot more dead people at my feet. Instead, I approached another, rather large fellow, and asked him if they needed another hand on deck. He laughed but took the time to look me up and down. He said, 'Wait here, *petit chat.*' He went to talk to a group of men and after a few minutes of whispering and laughing, they came down to the dock to meet me. That's where I met the Captain. His name was Darion Dogwood but everyone just called him Captain Dogwood. He was a large man with a big smile. But there was death in those eyes and I liked it. He shook my hand and spoke a bit in French to the big fellow I met earlier. They kept calling me *petit chat* and that name stuck. It means Little Cat," he laughed. "Their idea of humor."

"Little Cat, huh?" Wyatt snorted and wrote the name down on his notepad.

"Now don't go spreading that around, mate."

"Oh, it's written down now, Little Cat."

"Very funny. Anyway, Captain Dogwood took me on and taught me all I needed to know about being a proper Corsair, or Pirate to the nonprofessional," he laughed. "Dogwood helped me learn the new ways of the shipping industry. I was on that ship until all of them had either died or retired from the life. Then the day came when the ship was mine. I renamed her the Mystic Lady and we sailed for warmer waters. The place to be in those days, when piracy was really taking off, was the Barbary Coast off Africa. We raided and took ships but what was once a job for material goods changed a bit."

"What do you mean?"

"Now, don't go getting all offended, pal. This was a different time. But our main cargo turned out to be slaves. Christian slaves to be more precise."

"No…" Wyatt said in dismay.

"Yes. The Ottoman Empire required Christian slaves and we were the ones who supplied them to the empire." He looked at Wyatt and frowned "Look mate, I ain't proud of it but that's the truth of it. The Mystic Lady raided Christian villages, took off with her people, and delivered them to the masters of the Empire. That's how I won a name for myself on the seas and that's how many and more made a living. There were blokes from all over on the ships, once you became a part of the organization, you didn't have any national or religious ties. It was a kill or be killed world."

"I understand. I don't like it but I understand how it was," Wyatt said with a frown.

"Aye, it as a hard life but one I was perfectly suited for. My mates and I pillaged around the coasts all over. Our journeys on the sea took me farther than I'd ever dared to go. We went as far as Iceland and as far west as South America. Those were amazing times on the sea. We really were the masters of the sea by that time."

"You saw so much of the world. Did you ever dream it was this big?"

"The thing is I realized how small it was, actually. We passed ships on the sea at times and raised our flags to see who they were. Some we knew and some we didn't. But we were all people of the sea."

"Sounds like a brotherhood."

"It was. I remember when this country was being settled and we would follow the ships in to the bay to see the New World. It was amazing to watch the birth of a new land. There were people there, I know that, but they weren't world travelers like us. I guess it's easy to dismiss a people if they aren't living up to your standards. But that was the way of the world then. You either progressed with everyone else or you were taken over."

"Yep, sounds about right."

"Aye. We carried on all over the world until I was forced to say goodbye to the Mystic Lady."

"What happened?"

"She was an old ship. Too many repairs needed and so we sank her off the Barbary Coast. I acquired a new ship after that."

"How does one acquire a new ship?"

"Now that, that's a tale. Here's what happened… My mates and I were staying in Tunisia – fantastic country – and the ports were full to exploding with ships and other Corsairs. Pirates. Privateers. Whatever name suits you." He waved his hand to dismiss the issue. "There was a man,

well known to most, by the name of Captain Sanglant.
Captain Bloody in English. He was known for being hard
and I'd never had any dealings with him before this time.
But his ship, she was a beauty. I'd seen it a time or two and
she was bigger and faster than all the rest. Not sure where
he got it but it was the best on the seas at the time.So this
one night, we were drinking…"

"And whoring?"

"Of course. The women liked us. Oh boy, did they
ever. They liked our coins from all over the world and our
protection as well. But Sanglant, apparently, didn't like
whores. He liked virgins. Young ones."

"Eww."

"My mates and I left the watering hole and were
walking down the beautiful streets of Sfax when we heard
screams. Not the pleasant kind of screams, mind you, but
the kind that means there's trouble. We took off, drunk as
shit, towards the screams and found a few of Sanglant's
men with a clutch of young girls. These girls weren't no
whores. They were the young daughters of local merchants.
The girls were well groomed and, universally known to be
off limits. As a matter of courtesy, you see. But Sanglant's
men had stolen them from their homes and they were
dragging them kicking and screaming to their ship."

"What did you do?"

"Well, we sobered up right quick. Then we
followed in order to watch as they pulled those girls onto
the ship. Now, we didn't interfere right away. I mean, there
could've been something going on we didn't know about,
some arrangement made, that I didn't want to fuck up. You
didn't cross Sanglant unless you really had to."

"How could you not want to do something?"

"I did. But I needed to know for sure. I sent off two
of my men back to find the story. They came back with the
fathers of the girls. Both distraught and bleeding from
being used as punching bags. They explained they were in

debt to Sanglant and he took their daughters to settle the debt."

"Shit…"

"Aye. Shit it was. He was due his payment, of that I wouldn't dispute. But….I don't take kindly to men forcing themselves on women. There are plenty of willing women around who are more than happy to set your mast straight, so to speak." Wyatt laughed as Decker continued. "I found myself in a dilemma. Help the girls and risk an all-out fight with Sanglant? Or walk away and risk the guilt, knowing what he'd do to them?"

"You helped the girls, right?"

"Oy, who's telling this story?" He smiled at Wyatt. "Aye, I helped the girls. The boys and I told the merchants to stay quiet and hide as we stole onto the ship. There were six of us and who knows how many on board. But I figured they'd be busy….you know… with the girls. So, we were able to get on without anyone seeing us. But after that, it was quick work to cut the throats of those who were drinking and not keeping watch. We dropped them silently into the water and made our way to the Captain's cabin, where we heard the girls and the occasional shouts of the men.

"When we peeked through the panels, we saw a nasty sight, that's for sure. Two men had one of the girls-- she couldn't have been any older than twelve or thirteen-- naked and they were arguing over who'd take her first. The Captain had the other girl. He was real creepy. He was cutting off her dressing gown with his knife. He told her to stand real still or she'd be cut. Poor thing had to stand still for her own rape or else she'd get sliced.

"That's sick."

"Aye, It was. There was nothing for it really. We kicked the door down and flooded the room as fast as we could. Literally caught them with their cocks out." He let out a quick laugh, then chewed on his bottom lip. "One girl hadn't been hurt much. Just her pride really. Having to be naked in front of the men. But the other one, the one Sanglant had, she'd been hit a few times and…well…let's just say her virtue wasn't intact anymore."

"I thought you said he was cutting her dress off! He'd already….raped her?" Wyatt asked.

"Not himself, no. But…mate, I can skip the details if you want." Wyatt shook his head and motioned for him to continue. "As you say… he used the hilt of his sword to penetrate the girl. That's how he wasn't able to draw a proper blade on us when we rushed the room. It was inside of her."

"That's the most disgusting thing I've ever heard."

"No, it ain't. But it was despicable. I ran the Captain through with my sword and told the girls to help each other get dressed again. They didn't have much clothes left but, we found them bits of this and that to cover up with."

"You're such a good man, Decker." Wyatt said with a warm smile. Decker shrugged his shoulders, then smiled slyly.

"I got a ship out of the deal so it weren't all for altruistic reasons. By morning, the port didn't know what to think of the news that I'd dispatched the infamous Captain Sanglant, got his ship and renamed her the Dancing SeaWitch."

"Dancing SeaWitch? Where'd you get that name?"

"Don't know really. Maybe I always liked witches…" They both laughed and Wyatt wrote in his notepad. "But I kept that ship for a long, long time. I was Captain Chat for more years than I can count."

"Captain Chat. I like it."

"I sailed the SeaWitch into every known sea. It was a beauty of a ship to be sure. I finally had a home onboard that ship. But, like all things in my life, it had to end eventually."

"That's too bad. I'd give anything to see something like that."

"I'd give anything to see the SeaWitch again. But alas, she's sunk at the bottom of the harbor in New Orleans now. That was the last trip she made crossing the ocean in… let me think…early 1800's. We enjoyed a nice relationship with the new government of the New America and traded with her on a regular basis. I was among those who wanted to establish a new life there, so I travelled to New Orleans, knowing I wouldn't sail back. When I docked in port New Orleans, I was pretty shocked to find a familiar scent."

"Oh? Azul followed you?"

"No. Vasha was there. Or had been recently. I need to ask him about that some time. I'd be real curious to find out how he made it across the sea undetected by anyone. Even myself." He waved the thought away and concentrated on the story. "I had plenty of wealth so it was pretty easy to make my way there. I stayed in New Orleans for a while, partly because I wanted to see if Vasha would show up, honestly. And partly because it was what I knew. This was a whole new adventure for me. I had always travelled knowing I could turn around and go back, wherever back was, and be fine. But when I sunk my beloved SeaWitch in the port, I knew there was no going back."

"Why'd you sink the ship?"

"She was old, ancient really. I was pretty attached to her and decided, instead of seeing her stripped of parts, she deserved to die a death in the water. So I made sure she'd take on water and watched as the sea claimed the SeaWitch back. It was a fitting death for her."

"I see. Where'd you go after New Orleans? Did you find Vasha or the others?"

"Nope. Never found them. But I could feel them when they were close. And we were close on a number of occasions. But that's the thing-- I never knew if it'd be a fight with them and I didn't feel up to fighting with my brothers. When I smelled them or felt them getting close, I'd go the other way. My move to the New World was a fresh start for me. I was looking to put some years between wars, you know? But it wasn't long after my arrival I found out that wasn't gonna happen."

"Oh yes, we had our fair share of wars."

"Sadly, yes. There was the war with the Brits right after I landed…"

"The war of 1812?"

Decker snapped his fingers and pointed to Wyatt. "That'd be the one. What a mess. War became a joke by that time. All the pretty soldiers marching to a drummer in their colorful uniforms with their silly guns. Tell me, for fuck's sake, why did they ever do away with sword fighting?"

"They like guns nowadays."

"Aye. That brought down the caliber of warrior, in my opinion. That'll play well for Mela, I think."

"You really think this will come to an all-out war?" Wyatt asked. Decker reached for a cigarette and lit it. When he spoke, it was softer than before.

"Yes. This will be a war to remember. Maybe even the last war. Who knows?" He shrugged his shoulders and exhaled smoke. "All I know is Mela will end up on the front lines and I'm going to be right there with her."

"I wouldn't have it any other way."

"Neither would I." Decker pushed dark thoughts from his mind. He didn't want to think about the possibilities right now. This was a time for remembering and, hopefully, Wyatt would live long enough to tell the story to others who might want to know it.

"Did you fight in the Civil War?"

"Nar. I watched it though. Bloody fucking mess that was. By that time, my appetite for the slave trade was at an end. I didn't like being around any of them--the slaves or their masters. I found out this country has beautiful, untouched, countryside. I also found out the natives weren't very happy about the European invasion either. I spent some time with some Natives, what'd you call them? Indians?" Decker laughed and slapped his knee. "Indians….that's funny. Yeah, I learned the land and fiddled around with a few tribes, I don't remember what their names were 'cause I couldn't understand a damn thing they said. Lots of grunts and pointing. It was exhausting. I did find that I could get on just fine in a city though. If I stuck with going out at night, which I preferred, I did very well mingling with the folks. I found New York to be a hospitable place and I made my home there."

"I love New York! I went when I was a kid with my family. Beautiful place."

Decker nodded. "Aye. It was big and metropolitan, as they say. I had to get used to the Devil Wagons everywhere…"

"Devil Wagons?" Wyatt laughed.

"Cars! Those have got to be the worst possible invention ever made."

"But you call them Devil Wagons?" Wyatt laughed harder.

"Everybody called 'em that. They were right dangerous and there weren't no pretty streetlights or such things to help organize the blasted things. It was a mess, I tell you. But the life in the city was fast and loud. I loved it. I stuck near the ports because that's what I knew. I ran with a great group of chaps around that time. Darcy, Emmitt and Gene were my pals. They were a bunch of drunk bastards but great chaps all the same. It was Emmitt who gave me this hat." He handed the hat to Wyatt to inspect. "He and I were close pals. We shared an apartment for a while. He was the perfect roommate for me. Drunk from the time he woke up to whenever we called it a night and he knew where the best gambling games were."

"A match made in Heaven," Wyatt laughed.

"Emmitt, Darcy, Gene and I made it point to drink a lot and often. We enjoyed the cockfights, the horse races, but we loved to play card games the most. No matter how drunk Emmitt was, he was a master of the cards. He taught me how to play well and when I'd won enough money, I picked me up a Flivver."

"A what?"

"Flivver. It's what we called a cheap car. Emmitt taught me to drive, although, not very well. But man," he smiled at Wyatt, "We had some fun in those days."

"What happened to them? To Emmitt and Gene and," he checked his notes and read the last name. "Darcy?" Decker's smile turned sad and he took his hat in his hands again.

"Well, Darcy married some fat broad he met. Don't remember her name. When he told us he was getting married, we celebrated with him and got him drunk. But," he said, placing the hat on his head, "I knew that was that. Gene started working a proper job in the lumberyards upstate. Once he moved away, it was just Emmitt and me. We made plans to travel out west, maybe California, and go see the sights. We wanted to see the country. But Emmitt caught the flux, what you call it now? Tuber…"

"Tuberculosis?"

"Aye, that's the one. He was hospitalized and I spent many a night sitting in that damned place with him. He was pale and sickly at the end. I thought about ending it for him, you know? Going ahead and giving him a quick death. He was in a lot of pain and I hated to see it. But 'ol Emmitt, for all his bullshit, believed in the Bible and wouldn't take my mercy. He waited it out and sat in his chair every day, waiting for death. That's a hell of a thing to have to watch." Decker flicked his cigarette in the yard.

"The day he died, I was with him. He was in his bed, too weak to get up anymore. I sat with him, telling him stories about my life, kind of like what I'm doing now. He didn't believe me none though. At least," he looked at Wyatt, "I don't think he did. But he laughed in all the right places and seemed to like my little tales of adventure." Decker smiled.

"You were a good friend to him. I'm sure he appreciated it."

"Didn't change nothing though. At the end, he held my hand and looked at me. His eyes were dull like and his skin was as white as the sheets he'd been pissing in. He told me, 'You're a pain in my ass, Decker. I know you're not normal. I even think sometimes you're not even all together human. But I like you all the same. You've been a good friend.' Then he died. I left him there for the hospital folks to deal with. They buried him in a church somewhere, never went to see it."

"I'm sorry. I like your hat. Makes you look dapper," Wyatt said with a smile. Decker smiled and studied his bare feet.

"Death comes for everyone, maybe even me one day. I made a lot of mistakes in my life, but I did some good when I could."

"That's all anyone can do, Decker."

"Too right you are. Until now. Now I get a chance to be on the right side of a fight. Not by chance or by some ridiculous need for adventure, but because it's the right thing to do. That's why I'm staying. That's why I'm training Mela."

"She's lucky you're here. We're all lucky you're here actually."

"Ever since Emmitt died, I've just been roaming around. Made it out west to see California. Lived in the mountains for a long time. Wars came and went but I stayed out of them, until now. I was considering heading back to the Old World, back to Ireland maybe, when I felt it..."

"What? What'd you feel?"

"The magick Mela did to find my Sisters. That's a very unique and powerful magick because it's connected to them. And I think with us, me, Theo, and Vasha as well."

"If that's true, that means Azul knows too."

Decker nodded his head and rubbed a hand across his freshly shaven cheeks.

"Aye. That might be the case. Nothing we can do about it now. I have ideas, but I won't speak on it right now. I need to confer with my brothers before I do. There's a lot to do and I'm not sure how much time we've got to get it all done before..."

"Before?"

"Before everything changes. I feel it....a shift. Something is different and I can't put my finger on it," Decker lit another cigarette and stood up. "You need to do what I ask of you Wyatt. In this, you're our responsibility, but I can keep you safe. I can keep people safe now...if you listen to me. If you do what I tell you without being a right pain in my ass asking too many questions. Can you do that? Can you do what I ask of you to stay alive?"

Wyatt sat, stunned by the sudden serious tone in his friend. After a moment, he stood up and affirmed his choice.

"I can. As long as protecting people is what you want, I'll do it." Decker nodded once and clapped Wyatt on the back.

"Good. I've got to get a few things in order first and then, then my pal, we'll have a lot of work to do."

They looked up at the night sky, sprinkled with twinkling stars, in silence. Decker was confident, more than he'd ever been since coming to live at Mela's house. He knew Wyatt was afraid and that was good. But Decker wouldn't lose his friends if he could help it. He'd train them to fight and the rest, he'd protect. Even if it meant his life.

He had memories of love and memories of dead friends that once shared his life. But these people, including his brothers, were alive and needed him. Those that Mela cared about, who cared about her, were his responsibility now more than ever. He knew Theo would be willing to help him, for the sake of all the innocents, of that he was certain. Vasha was…unpredictable. But he could be coerced into certain tasks with the right motivation. He would need to find what that was.

He wished Wyatt goodnight and laughed when his friend showed him a sketch of Decker with his sword. It was a pretty good likeness and he complimented him on it. It pleased him more than he would ever let on that Wyatt cared as much as he did. He was a good man and a good friend. He wanted him to survive what was coming. Desperately. Decker was willing to do anything to make sure that happened.

As he walked from the porch and felt the cooler fall air blow, he knew his brother was near. Silently as ever, Theo stepped from the shadows and fell in step beside him. They walked toward the shed where Vasha kept house.

"We have plans to make, brother?" Theo asked.

Decker smiled and looked up into his brother's yellow eyes. They were alight with purpose and full of excitement.

"Aye. We have plans to make."

They entered the shed together.

Coming Winter 2014 from Solstice Publishing…

EARTH'S MAGICK
BOOK 2
~WATER~

Chapter 1

Mela rolled over in bed and almost cried out in pain. Every muscle in her body screamed when she tried to reach for her cell phone to turn the alarm off. After a few unsuccessful attempts, she finally managed to reach it and hit the right button.

"Oww," Mela groaned. Sitting up was harder than it should have been. Every muscle in her body, including her hands, burned with the slightest movement. It was Saturday. Normally, she'd sleep late, enjoy a lazy morning sipping coffee, and watch television. Her life wasn't normal anymore.

"Hey….you up yet, poppet? Time to get to work. Time to bleed!" Decker laughed as he gave her bedroom door a few hard thumps with his fist.

"I'm up. I'm up. Stop it…. Shit." Swinging her legs onto the floor was difficult to do since Mela was trying very hard not to use her abdominal muscles. She shuffled like an old woman to the bathroom and closed the door behind her. Every morning for the past two weeks was the same. Decker made her train before work and after work. She was exhausted.

Since it was Saturday, they would be training off and on all day. He made her run as well. Mela hated to run. He forced her to do sit-ups, pull-ups, pushups, yoga, and finally combat training. She thought it would be more fun than it really was. The people in movies made learning new stuff look way too easy. This was not easy.

After an obscene amount of exercise, Decker would toss her a wooden sword and make her slowly go through drills. Her muscles were so sore the practice sword felt like lead in her hands. With painfully slow movements, Decker would stand directly in front of Mela and she was to mimic his every move. She thought she would never look as graceful as he did when he sliced his sword through the air.

Like a cat, he would bend and stretch his body and he looked so damn strong while he did it. She watched his muscles flex in his arms and his back. His power and grace were hard to watch and not get lost in. His balance was the only thing Mela seemed to be able to mirror with little difficulty. There were times when he would shift his weight from one foot to the next and she was thankful she could follow him.

It wasn't simply the workouts or the sword play that hurt her. It was what happened after all of that. When Decker took her sword and turned to face her with his mischievous grin, she knew he was about to hit her. The first time he hit her, it hurt like hell. It caught her off guard and she fell flat on her ass. Learning to block was her first lesson and that was why her arms were so sore. His punches, although he denied it, were full of power. If that was a light punch, then she never wanted to be at the receiving end of real one.

Mela washed her face and picked up dirty clothes from the floor. She sniffed them and decided they weren't dirty enough to wash yet, so she put them on. A bit of dirt, and what looked like dried blood were on the front of the t-shirt, but other than that, it would work. She looked at herself in the mirror and, despite being exhausted, she saw she'd dropped a few pounds and a healthy glow was in her cheeks. As she brushed her teeth, Mela found something to tie her hair back with. The last time she forgot to do that, Decker grabbed a fist full of her brown locks and took her to the ground. Pulling hair really is an effective tactic in a fight.

She felt somewhat ready as she made her way into the living room and started turning on lights. Decker sat on the kitchen counter eating something that resembled a sandwich. But it dripped with too much sauce and he made a mess. Decker had discovered hot sauce and now he drowned everything with it. He hopped off the counter when he saw Mela and shoved the remnants of the sandwich in his mouth.

"You ready?" His words were muffled but she nodded to him. Together, they walked outside into the early morning. The sun wasn't really up yet. The sky was gray and a slight morning chill was in the air. Mela inhaled the smell of fall and memories of her childhood flooded her mind. This was the time of year children were going back to school, she thought. She remembered this early morning smell of fall as she walked to the bus stop. Everything was so calm and normal to her back then.

"Oy...catch," Decker tossed her a wooden sword and she deftly caught it in her right hand. Despite being sore, she really enjoyed these lessons with him. Vasha would make his way out to watch as well, after he slept late and ate a big breakfast, of course. Surprised, Mela thought they wouldn't be fighting this early, but she took her stance and bent her knees, readying herself for the fight. Decker gave her a look and shook his head. "Not yet," he said as he stretched his muscular arms across his chest. She relaxed and stood, wary this was some sort of test. Or worse, he'd attack her with no warning.

Mela began stretching, keeping a close eye on him as she did. After a few moments, she heard footsteps crunching on the fallen leaves. Theo and Bear walked casually together towards them. For a moment, it seemed as though they were having a silent conversation. However, since she was keeping one eye on Decker, she couldn't tell before Bear and Theo parted ways. Theo crouched down just outside of the designated fighting area. Bear galloped to Mela and leaned his large body against her in greeting. She rubbed his head and looked at Decker, questioning the change in program.

"Time for a bit of a change up. As my brother has pointed out, if I'm to train you, I've got to train your familiar as well." Bear watched Decker, his bright brown eyes attentive and ready. Mela frowned and bit her bottom lip.

"You won't hurt him, will you?" Mela asked. Decker threw his hands in the air in frustration.

"No, no more than I hurt you. But he's gotta learn, Mela. He's your familiar and Theo's been teaching him a few things as well. That right, brother?" Mela turned and Theo nodded at her.

"All is well. He understands much and is eager to fight by your side." Theo's soft voice made her feel a lot more secure. She knew Decker wouldn't hurt her, per se, but she trusted Bear's life to Theo over anyone else.

She turned and took her fighting position with Bear by her side. Decker smiled and made a feint toward her. Mela stepped back deftly, wooden sword at the ready, when he did. Bear took two steps back and circled behind Decker. Mela smiled, seeing the plan, and decided to go on the offensive. She made a swift strike that barely missed Decker's chest and he hopped back, laughter in his eyes.

"You can't get me….Ouch!" Bear had Decker's leg in his jaws. His bite wasn't hard enough to break the skin but was firm enough that he could toss his head back and forth and let loose a low growl as he did. That was all Mela needed.

She slid on the ground toward him, as he'd often told her to do, and gave his shins a solid *whack!* with the side of the sword. Bear let go of Decker and Mela was once again on her feet. Decker was rubbing both of his legs and cursing up a storm. She smiled, knowing she'd regret the smugness later, but she couldn't help it. It was the first time she'd been able to gain the upper hand against him.

It felt good.

About the Author...

Mel Massey is the author of the Earth's Magick series and other paranormal stories. Her husband is an active duty soldier in the United States Army, which keeps Mel's family moving around constantly. Mel is a practicing Pagan and an avid bibliophile.

Visit www.melmassey.com for book news and visit the forums to chat with other Earth's Magick readers.

Other Solstice Shadows books you might enjoy...

Earth's Magick, Book 1 ~ Earth~
By: Mel Massey

Life in Trinity Hills, Texas goes from normal to deadly for Mela Malone. Whenever Mela falls asleep, a mysterious creature, called The Hag, tries to kill her. What begins as dabbling in protective spells from an ancient Grimoire, leads to her initiation into an ancient order of warrior witches known as the Elementai.
Mela learns war is coming with The Darkness and the Hag is only one of the evil creatures in its service. As an Elementai, Mela learns it's her duty to find four part-human sisters who can help defeat the evil that threatens to return to the world. With every new discovery, Mela uncovers ancient secrets that complicate her quest further.
As war approaches, everyone must make a choice - fight with the Elementai for all life on Earth, or fight for The Darkness...

Getaway

By: Mel Massey

When Lisa goes to visit her parents, she comes home to an empty house. Or so she thinks. As a storm rages outside, Lisa tries to get away from something unknown that's hiding in the shadows.

Magick & Moonlight
By: Marie Lavender

Messing with free will is always a bad idea…

Ethan Hamilton moves to a lazy little town in Oregon, hoping to escape his demons. But, instead he discovers a woman dancing nude in the moonlight. This woman who claims she is a witch dazzles him with her sensual presence. He thinks she's crazy, but what if she's not?

Jessie Anderson has been taught that her kind hides who they really are. And she has a problem on her hands. Someone knows her secret and she has to do all she can to protect herself. What other choice does she have? Jessie casts a love spell on a good man, a man with whom she can't fight her attraction. The spell doesn't work quite as planned – she ends up falling for Ethan.

To top it off, Ethan's treatment of her, his "love", is so addictive. Deep down, she knows the spell will wear off, and yet his feelings seem genuine. It's just a spell…right?

Visit Solstice Shadows online bookstore for more titles:
http://solsticepublishing.com/bookstore/